THE DA

Books in the Series

The House of Fear

THE DANGEROUS MAN

IBN-E SAFI

Translated by

Taimoor Shahid

RANDOM HOUSE INDIA

Published by Random House India in 2011
1

Copyright © The Estate of Ibn-e-Safi
Translation Copyright © Taimoor Shahid 2011

Random House Publishers India Private Limited
Windsor IT Park, 7th Floor, Tower-B, A-1
Sector 125, Noida 201301, UP

Random House Group Limited
20 Vauxhall Bridge Road
London SW1V 2SA
United Kingdom

978 81 8400 118 1

This book is sold subject to the condition that it shall not, by way of trade or otherwise, be lent, resold, hired out, or otherwise circulated without the publisher's prior consent in any form of binding or cover other than that in which it is published and without a similar condition including this condition being imposed on the subsequent purchaser.

Typeset by SwaRadha Typesetting, New Delhi

Printed and bound in India by Replika Press Pvt. Ltd.

For Farhan and Billu bhai,
who invited me to *Ibn-e Safi*
by locking away
their precious Imran-series collection
in a private chest,
tempting me to secretly arrange for copies of
my own.
And for Bari, my grandmother,
who was the foremost—
and sometimes the sole—
supporter of my literary pursuits.

Contents

Mysterious Screams — 1

A Dangerous Man — 103

Acknowledgements — 205

MYSTERIOUS SCREAMS

Chapter 1

MOODY, THE SON OF a famous American billionaire, was a romantic young man and had travelled to this faraway, magical land ostensibly to look after his father's business. But, in reality, it was his fascination with the mysterious East that had brought him here. A dreamer since childhood, fantasizing about life in far-off, exotic lands was second nature to him.

He would often get drunk and drive around the streets and alleyways of the city. Every time he went on these drunken jaunts he made sure to pass by the old and decrepit neighbourhoods of town at least once. Evenings were best suited for these drives. The last rays of the setting sun, gleaming on the rundown walls of old buildings, created an air of mystery, and at these times, Moody felt his spirit hovering around these ancient walls.

One day he was roaming around the roads of Alamgiri Sirai. The sun had already set, and darkness was slowly eclipsing twilight. He drove very slowly through a narrow, deserted alleyway, so slowly that even a child could have opened the door of his car and climbed in.

Lost in thought, Moody was softly humming a tune when he was startled by the sound of someone quickly opening and closing the rear door of his car. He turned around but could not see anything in the dark. He quickly switched on the cabin light. His hands trembled.

'Switch it off...for God's sake...please switch it off,' came a girl's quavering voice. She had addressed him in English but her accent was definitely Eastern. Moody promptly switched off the light. 'Please save me!' the girl seated at the back said.

'Okay...okay,' Moody said, nodding quickly. He was completely baffled. He sped out of the alleyway.

Even though he was quite drunk he knew he had spoken too soon. He had agreed to help this unknown young woman without a thought, and now he had no idea how he was going to save her. Nor did he know what on earth he was saving her from. After some time he asked, 'How can I help you?'

'Please take me to a safe place, I am in danger!' she replied.

'Shall I take you to the police station?' asked Moody.

'No, no!' There was fear in the girl's voice.

'Why not?' he asked. 'What is a better place than a police station if you are in danger?'

'You don't understand...it's a matter of honour!'

'I have no idea what you're talking about. Anyway, I can drop you off wherever you want.'

'Oh God! What should I do!' the girl mumbled to herself. Her seductive, dreamy voice exhilarated him. It carried in its lilt ancient secrets and mysteries.

'Why don't you go home?' Moody asked.

'Going home at this time would be like inviting death.'

'You say strange things!'

'Please save me! I feel that I can trust you...because you're a foreigner.'

'What's the matter?'

'Not something that you will easily believe...'

'What do I do then, tell me?' Faced with her plea, Moody felt helpless.

'Take me to your place...but only if there are no dogs around. You see, I am scared of dogs.'

'Take you home?' Moody swallowed. He felt that his most cherished dreams were about to come true. After a few moments of silence, he said, 'I have dogs, but they are not dangerous.' He turned the car towards his house and asked the girl, 'What sort of danger are you in?'

'It can only be explained at leisure,' she said. 'If I start telling you here you will laugh it off. I wouldn't be surprised if you asked me to get out of the car.'

Moody didn't say a word. This strange but beautiful woman thrilled him to the bone. He remembered stories of the ancient East that he had read in his childhood. The mysterious, beautiful women of these tales had haunted his dreams. He longed to switch on the cabin light and take a long look at her. What an enchanting face! What hypnotic eyes! He thought he saw a halo around her head. He wanted to switch on the light to reassure himself that he was not imagining these things, but could not muster the courage to do so. The girl had stopped talking, but her voice still echoed in Moody's ears.

They reached Moody's house and drove through the gate into the compound. Instead of parking his car in the garage Moody drove straight to the porch. A few moments later, the woman of his dreams was standing before him. She was a young Eastern woman with very refined features. She wore simple, traditional clothes that suggested a working class background. She held a small leather briefcase in her hand. Moody hesitantly asked her to sit down and pointed to the sofa. She sat down. Moody waited for her to say something, but she kept staring at the floor in silence. It seemed as though she had forgotten why she had come there. Moody waited. After she had been silent for quite a while he asked, 'What can I do for you now?'

The girl gave a start as if he had suddenly appeared out of thin air. 'Oh...' she said, licking her lips. 'I've given you a lot of trouble!'

'No, not at all. It's all right,' Moody said. 'Would you like something to drink?'

'No, thank you,' the girl said, placing the leather briefcase on the floor. She was silent again.

Moody was getting restless now. In an attempt to get her to talk about her situation, he finally said, 'I will try to help you in every possible way.'

'I don't know what to say to you or where to start,' the girl replied.

'Please say something!' Moody said irritably. His intoxication was dissipating, and he always became a little petulant when this happened.

'Just…give me a moment,' the girl said. She picked up the leather briefcase and placed it on the sofa. 'I am very grateful to you for bringing me here. May I ask you for another favour?'

'Please do tell me,' Moody said, lighting a cigarette.

'I want to entrust one of my belongings to your care for a few days,' the girl said. She opened the briefcase and took out a small ebony box. Moody's eyes widened in wonder when he saw the box—it was inlaid with priceless jewels.

'This jewellery box belonged to an ancient queen of our land,' the girl said, extending the box to Moody. 'Please keep it with you for a few days.'

'Why…why do you want to entrust it to me?'

'I live by myself. I have no family, and some people have their eyes on this box. They have been after me for quite some time. I had a narrow escape today.'

'But where did you find it?'

'Surely you don't think I have stolen it from someone?'

'That's not what I meant,' Moody replied quickly. 'It's just that…'

'…by my appearance I do not look like someone who can own such a casket?' the girl asked with a slight smile.

'You misunderstood me…'

'Let me explain everything to you,' she said, taking a deep breath. 'I am the sole survivor of an ancient royal family of this land. I inherited this jewellery box.'

'Really?' Moody shifted restlessly. It seemed as though his dream world was materializing right before his eyes.

'Yes, truly. Please get this thought out of your head that I stole it from somewhere.'

'You are being unfair,' Moody protested. 'I never meant that... Of course, I will take care of it, Your Royal Highness.' He found himself addressing her with a royal title.

'Thank you very much. However, I must warn you: it is quite possible that you may be harmed because they will try and seize it from you.'

'Impossible!' Moody said scoffing. 'I can shoot a bird in flight. No one dare set foot in my compound without my permission!'

'You can still change your mind.' the girl said, looking enquiringly into his eyes.

'I have made up my mind. I will help you,' he said. 'When will you take it back?'

'When things get better. That is why I asked you to understand the situation fully before offering to help.'

'Don't worry. I won't ask you another question. You can decide as you please.'

'I don't want anything from you except that you safeguard this box for me for a few days.'

'I am ready to do that. When will I see you again?'

'That depends on the circumstances.'

'Okay... How will you get back? They might be lurking outside.'

'It doesn't matter. They can't harm me any more.'

'Why? Weren't you anxious about it a little while ago?'

'Of course I was, but the source of my anxiety won't be with me any more.'

'What if they abduct and torture you?'

'I am strong.'

'But why don't you inform the police?'

'Oh! Even that could lead to my ancestral inheritance being taken away from me. If the government gets a hint of this, they will want the Ministry of Archaeology to keep the box.'

'Hmm...' Moody said in agreement. 'That's true.'

'It is a difficult situation. I can't inform the police, and I can't keep it with me... If I do either, I will be in trouble. I suppose silence is my only option.'

'You are right. I promise to safeguard it for you, Your Royal Highness.'

'Thank you very much.'

'May I ask your name? Where do you live?'

'Name...my name is Durdana...and my address... no, I can't tell you...you won't understand...I am in trouble...we will meet occasionally.'

'That's all right. I won't force you.' He was silent for a while, and then he said, 'Would you like to join me for dinner?'

'No, thank you.' The girl stood up. 'Do you mind seeing me to the gate?' she asked.

Moody wanted her to stay a little longer, but he couldn't gather the courage to ask her. He had an inexplicable desire to be commanded by the girl and to obey her as a slave.

He walked her to the gate and stood there gazing at her until she disappeared from his sight. Moody had offered to drive her wherever she wanted to go, but she had refused. After she left, Moody continued staring into the darkness. He walked inside after a while. He drank a few pegs of whisky in quick succession and then carried the jewellery box to his bedroom. The gems studded on its casing glittered blindingly. Already lost in a fantasy world, he didn't try to open it. He was transported back in time. He imagined that he was the bodyguard of a royal princess, and that he was waging war against her foes.

He was already quite drunk and so he actually began fighting the phantom enemies of his imaginary princess. His first punch landed on the wall, the second on a table, and the third—in all likelihood—on his own head. He created such a ruckus that soon all his servants had gathered around him and were looking on in wonder.

Chapter 2

IMRAN WAS SITTING IN his office browsing through a file. Imran? Working in an office? Indeed, it was unbelievable. But the poor guy had not been able to shake off the government's insistence that he work for them. After Li Yu Ka's arrest his identity was in danger of becoming known. Then the House of Fear case had caused a stir. Both these cases had become so prominent that his identity could no longer remain a secret. Imran's father Rehman Sahib, who was the Director General of the Intelligence Bureau, could hardly believe in the abilities of his half-crazy son. He thought of him as ox-witted and stupid, among many other things.

The Honourable Interior Minister had invited Imran and had offered him a good post in the Intelligence Bureau, and Imran had not been able to say no to him. But Imran had also put forth some conditions which had been accepted. His principal suggestion had been that he would investigate crimes on his own. Then came the condition that he would have his own section. He would report directly to the Director General, and would not be answerable to anyone except him. He would not necessarily hire new people for his team; whenever he found someone from the Bureau that he could use, he would request a transfer. His team would not exceed ten people.

Imran offered his services after the conditions were accepted. But Rehman Sahib was very embarrassed when he learnt that Imran had been selecting utterly useless and lazy men for his workforce. He had selected four until now and all four of them were considered completely useless in the Bureau. No one liked to have them in their section and they had spent their lives shuttling from transfer to transfer. Put together, their personalities came to naught—thin-bodied weaklings, lazy, good-for-nothing procrastinators that they were. Imran knew what was coming and it was as he had expected: Rehman Sahib called him to his office and admonished him severely.

'If it were up to me I'd have you thrown out this very moment,' he said.

'I want an official explanation of this sentence,' Imran said very politely. This irritated Rehman Sahib even more. Then he suddenly realized that he was not talking to his son but to a subordinate officer.

'Why have you chosen such good-for-nothing people?' he asked, controlling his anger.

'Only because I don't want anyone to be a good-for-nothing in this department,' was Imran's reply.

Rehman Sahib gritted his teeth but did not say anything. Imran's reply was enough to make anyone speechless. He had to shut up because Imran had settled matters with the Interior Minister directly. Some people mocked Imran's procedures while others looked upon them with amazement. But Imran, indifferent to public opinion, continued to do his job.

The file that lay before him at this moment consisted of documents related to cases in which the Bureau had not achieved any success. This file had resurfaced on his desk because new light had been shed on an old case. It was an unresolved ten-year-old case. The Intelligence Bureau had been unable to get to the bottom of things. This case hadn't been of much consequence ten years ago. But now—now it had taken such an astonishing turn that the whole city was stunned. The case was strange. Ten years ago someone had murdered the city's famous aristocrat Nawwab Hashim in his bedroom. But now, ten years later, Nawwab Hashim had been seen alive—a flesh-and-bone man. He had returned from a long journey.

Imran closed the file and put it on one side of the table. He took out a pack of chewing gum from his pocket and ripped off its wrapper.

Meanwhile Superintendent Fayyaz's attendant entered and said, 'Sahib sends his salaam.'

'Wa alaikum salaam, convey my salaam to him,' Imran said, leaned back in his chair, and closed his eyes. The orderly was baffled. The man had been trained during the British Raj and in those days the only purpose of sending a salaam was to summon the subordinate. When a British officer wanted to summon a subordinate, he would send his salaam to him through his orderlies. Today, however, Fayyaz's orderly was completely bewildered by Imran's 'wa alaikum salaam'.

He stood beside Imran's table for a while and looked around in perplexity. Then he retraced his steps. He could not find the courage to convey Imran's 'Convey my salaam to him' to Fayyaz. Instead, he told Fayyaz's personal assistant about it. This personal assistant was a girl. She laughed for a few moments and then conveyed Imran's reply to Fayyaz. He was extremely angry. He was Imran's friend but ever since Imran had joined the Bureau, Fayyaz had started treating him like his subordinate. This time he called the attendant and told him, 'Go tell Imran that Sahib is calling him.'

The attendant left. After a while Imran entered the room.

'Sit.' Fayyaz pointed to a chair. Imran sat. Fayyaz stared at him for some time and then said, 'Friendship is a different matter. In the office you will have to respect protocol.'

'I don't understand. What are you saying?'

'I am your boss.'

'Oh, wow!' Imran said, making a face. 'Who the hell told you that you were my boss?! Look, Mister Fayyaz! I have my own independent section and I am its sole in-charge. And I am directly answerable to the Director General, understand!'

'I see,' Fayyaz said, taking a deep breath. He had softened a little. Perhaps he was reminded of the 'miracle' of his promotion. He had only been an Inspector at first, but had rapidly risen to the rank of superintendent in the space of a mere five years. In his heart of hearts he knew that Imran had done a lot for these promotions. 'Look, what I mean to say is that you shouldn't behave like a fool in the office.'

'Where is it written that there is no place for fools in this office?'

'Oh, just stop it! I want to talk to you about an important matter.'

'I think that my foolishness is very important too, since it is only because of this foolishness that I've reached this position. By the way, I know that you want to talk about Nawwab Hashim.'

'Have you understood the case fully?'

'Yes, I have. But I can't understand why he was declared murdered. There were a thousand reasons why it could have also been considered a suicide.'

'For example?' Fayyaz asked, looking at him meaningfully.

'For example, the shot was fired at his face. The gun was a 12 mm and the shell SG—the face was completely destroyed. It was so disfigured that identification was difficult. He was identified only because of his clothes and other clues. The gun was found lying beside him and there is also proof that the shot was fired at close quarters. The post-mortem report says that the distance of the muzzle from his face could not have been more than a hand span.'

'To hell with it!' Fayyaz said, slamming his hand on the table. 'That wretch is alive. He says that he left home without telling anyone because he had to. He was away touring southern continents all this time and now he has returned. Whose corpse was found in his bedroom? Nawwab Hashim doesn't have a clue.'

'Wait a minute,' Imran said, raising his hand. 'So that means that the night the corpse was discovered he must have been home during the day?'

'Of course.'

'So then he left home at night, and the incident happened that very night. A man wearing Nawwab Hashim's nightsuit was shot in his bedroom.'

'Yes, that is it,' Fayyaz said, lighting a cigarette.

Imran thought for a few moments. Then he said, 'What does he have to say about that corpse?'

'His response is clear. He says, what can I say? It is my family's fault. They didn't identify the corpse correctly.'

'But what was the purpose behind disappearing like this without letting anyone know?'

'Mad love!' Fayyaz said, sighing heavily.

'Oh. Well, then I can't do anything really!' Imran said gravely. 'It's a famous saying that the travails of love can crush even a demon's soul.'

'Imran, be serious!'

'I am very serious! If he hadn't run away like this, he would have really fallen in love with someone.'

'Stop spouting nonsense. He was heartbroken because he had been disappointed in love. That's why he had to leave.'

'Have you no fear of God, Fayyaz! It was wartime. And it was a norm in those days for people to register themselves in the army when they had been disappointed in love. Holidaying was not the norm in those circumstances.'

'Don't annoy me!' Fayyaz said irritably. 'Go, get lost!'

Imran stood up silently and left the room. The telephone in his room was ringing. He picked up the receiver.

'Hello...yes, who else can it be but Imran...who... Moody, what is it, at least tell me something...okay, enough...don't irritate me...fine I'm coming right now.'

After hanging up, he turned towards the door where one of his torpid subordinates was standing and staring at him; his face pale, cheeks sucked in, hair unkempt.

'Hmm... What's the news?' Imran asked him.

'Sir, I have gathered some information.'

'Well done! You see! Initially you used to say that information runs away from you but now...now you are getting quite good. Shortly you'll become a sergeant. But always remember one thing: the scientific way of fooling someone is to act like a fool oneself, understand?'

'Yes sir! I understand fully. Anyway, now please listen to the report. Nawwab Hashim hasn't left the haveli. Today a red car came to the haveli twice. A boy sang a cappella film songs for half an hour in the compound of the haveli. Then at eleven o'clock a very frisky and naughty sweeper woman entered the haveli. She had a raised black mole on her left cheek. Oval face, intoxicating eyes, height between four and a half and five.'

'What...you are really progressing!' Imran cried, delighted. 'Well done! Observe everything very attentively. What was the number of the car?'

'I didn't pay attention to that, sir.'

'Don't worry, everything will be fine eventually. Okay, now go, your duty there resumes at four.'

Imran got out, took his black coupe from the shed, and drove towards Moody's bungalow. Moody was one of his best friends. When Imran reached the house, he found Moody drinking. He was drunk almost all the time. Upon seeing Imran he stood up and saluted him in the traditional manner. He was extremely fond of Eastern social norms and always tried to adopt them with Easterners.

Chapter 3

MOODY HAD STARTED HIS story. Imran was listening intently.

'So she left the jewel casket with me,' he continued, 'and the same day some people tried to enter my bungalow.'

'Were you awake?'

'I had been up all night. I saw them. Fired a few shots and they fled in fear. But the very next day, and for long after, a line of strangers was always outside my door. I saw faces that utterly surprised me; some of them had come for employment, some wanted to know about the American way of life, and some were here only to befriend me! Around ten to fifteen people came to me in this manner. Nobody used to come here before. Then a very strange man came one evening. He said that he was the owner of my bungalow. Let me make clear that I've rented this bungalow through an agency. And this strange newcomer said to me that he doesn't trust any agency's people! "I want to see the condition of the bungalow from the inside!" Just think about it, dear Imran; of course, I was not stupid enough to allow him inside, especially under these circumstances. So my dear friend, won't you join me for a drink…'

'No, thanks. Yes, so then what happened?'

'You know that I am a mysterious man myself,' Moody said, enjoying every word of the tale. 'Who can make a fool out of me? I dismissed him!' Moody topped up the second glass and brought it to his lips.

'Did the girl come again?' Imran asked.

'Ah! This is the most painful part of the story, my friend!' Moody said, gulping down the entire contents of the glass in a single breath and slamming it on the table. 'She came...this is about ten days ago...she came and said, "I don't know what to do. How do I keep such a thing with myself? I am a friendless girl. My head will indeed be chopped off!" I asked her why she didn't sell it to some sensible person. This way her financial condition would also improve. After a little hesitation she agreed. I made her an offer of twenty-five thousand rupees. She said that was a lot. In her opinion it didn't have much value. How innocent she is! Ah! Imran dear, she still...! Ah! I forcefully gave her twenty-five thousand rupees... And all this time I had to be up all night with a revolver to guard the jewel box!'

'Come, where is it, let me see it,' Imran said.

'Wait...I'll show it to you...' Suddenly Moody's mood changed. His upper lip twitched and his eyes seemed to drip blood. Imran observed this rapid transformation in his emotions with wonder, but did not say anything. Moody stood up with a start and went into another room. Imran waited silently.

Suddenly he heard a din in the other room, and a servant came running to the room where he was seated.

Panting, he said to Imran, 'Sahib, save Moody Sahib!'

'What happened?' Imran jumped up. The servant pointed to the door of the room and ran towards it himself. Imran reached the room in a flash. Moody was in a bizarre state. A couple of his servants were holding him down. He was banging his head with a black box.

'Move away...move away!' he bellowed as he hit his head with the box.

Imran seized the box from his hands with much difficulty, and somehow the servants pushed Moody onto a sofa. Imran weighed the box in his hand, his eyes fixed on the jewels that studded the four corners of the box.

'This is it,' Moody roared, getting up from the sofa, 'this is it!'

'Get back to your senses, son, or I'll dunk your head in a bucket of cold water!' Imran said.

'I am completely in my senses!' Moody bellowed. 'Ever since I paid for these jewels I haven't been able to sleep properly at night! Do you understand me or should I yell some more?'

'You go to sleep now,' Imran said. 'We'll talk some other time.'

'What...now you won't help me either?'

'Talk sense if you want help!'

'Come now,' Moody said, striking his forehead, 'ever since I purchased this, not a single suspicious person has come here. No one has tried to seize it.'

'Hmm...' Imran said, taking a deep breath. 'Why didn't you tell me that before? I understand what's going on now.'

'You understand, right?'

'Yes, and if you continue to remain besotted with the mysterious then you will soon be penniless. In fact, I am afraid that soon you will seek recourse in the occult—buying amulets, charmed cords, and rings!'

'What are these things?'

'Nothing. Do you know the address of that girl?'

'She lives in Alamgiri Sirai.'

'Alamgiri Sirai is a very large locality!' Imran said.

'But now please tell me what I should do... I don't care about the twenty-five thousand rupees! I... Ah! How can I believe that she's a charlatan! She seems to be the kind of woman who has been alive for a thousand years... Have you read Rider Haggard's novel *She*?'

'Moody kay bacche...your brain has gone to mush!' Imran said, waving a fist in his face.

'No! I have more sense than you,' Moody said, waving him away.

'Have you had these jewels on the box inspected by someone?'

'Yes, I have! I don't care that I've been fooled. Ah! It's a calamity; how can I think of her as a charlatan! No! She is a princess!'

'Oh, shut up. You idiot! Did you even try meeting her again?'

'No. I couldn't gather the courage.'

Imran could only look at him compassionately.

'What is the value of these stones?' he asked Moody.

'Not stones...call them replicas,' Moody said. 'They are not worth more than a hundred and fifty rupees!'

'Oh Moody! May God have mercy on you!' Imran said and Moody made the sign of the cross. After a brief silence Imran said, 'Do you have the complete address of the girl?'

'I do, but what will you do?'

'Nothing! Of course she would not be there any more or perhaps she has never been there to begin with!'

'Ah! Then you too are trying to prove that she is a fraud!'

'Now stop talking nonsense, or I'll shoot you!'

'Shoot me! But I won't believe she is a fraud! She walks so gently. Like a spring breeze! The pink glow of the morning rises in her cheeks! Languorous evenings yawn in her tresses!'

'And my slap will beat the living daylights out of you! I am telling you I need her address and nothing more!'

'The yellow house near the half-minaret. That's it. I don't know anything beyond that!'

Imran frowned at Moody and said, 'Why did you call me when you are not even bothered about the money you've lost!'

'Dear Imran! I just want you to prove that she is not a fraud! Since you are a government official, I'll take your word for it! But if someone else were to say that, then it is possible that I wouldn't believe him.'

'Okay, son!' Imran said, nodding. 'For your sake I will demand the establishment of a Love Affairs Section in the Investigation Bureau… And you could have just told me all of this over the phone!'

'Ah! How could I have explained all this to you! Operators eavesdrop on conversations over the phone! I don't want anyone to think of Princess Durdana as an imposter. Ah…princess!'

'Princess, my foot! I am going. If you waste my time again, I'm going to waste you! I am taking this jewellery box with me.'

'No way!' Moody grabbed Imran's hand. 'I will guard it until my last breath! Even if the princess's enemies follow me up to the Mount of Qaf!'

'Your disease is incurable!' Imran said, shaking his head in despair, and left the room after putting the jewellery box on the table. Moody called after him, letting out a volley of bloodcurdling screams.

Chapter 4

IMRAN'S COUPE STOPPED IN front of Hashim's haveli. It was an old style building, but the front lawn was modern and the wall surrounding it, almost as tall as a man, also looked like a later addition. Imran left the car outside and walked through the gate. A garden path went straight from the entrance to the verandah of the haveli. As soon he stepped onto the gravelly red path, a huge dog appeared out of nowhere and stood before Imran.

'I know,' Imran muttered in a low voice, 'how could the dominion be complete without you! Now, please step out of my way.'

The dog was very strange. He made no sound, nor did he move forward. Imran heard a voice calling the dog, 'Raygi! Raygi!' The voice came nearer and a man emerged from the begonia shrubs nearby, moving towards Imran. He was a middle-aged man with a strong build. A strange sense of desolation flashed in his eyes. He had a round face, devoid of any facial hair. The hair was a greying mess. His lips were very thin and he had a heavy jaw. He was wearing a pair of sharkskin pants and a white silk shirt.

'Yes?' he asked, staring at Imran.

'I would like to meet Nawwab Sahib.'

'Why do you want to meet him?'

'I have to discuss varieties of manure with him.'

'Varieties of manure?' the man repeated in astonishment and then said, 'But, pray, who are you?'

'I am a news reporter.'

'Again these news reporters!' he muttered in a low voice. Then he said loudly, 'Look, mister, I don't have time.'

'But I have a lot of time,' Imran said seriously. 'Actually, I wanted to ask you whose corpse was it ten years ago? Will you kindly shed some light on this riddle?'

'For God's sake, please leave!' he said, exasperated. 'I don't know anything about it! If I had known about this bizarre incident, perhaps I would have never bothered to return!'

'I am utterly surprised,' Imran said, 'at how speedy your departure was, that you couldn't get the news of your own murder!'

'Look, son, I am very troubled. Come some other time when I'm not preoccupied,' Nawwab Hashim said.

'Okay, then at least tell me: how do you feel in these circumstances?'

'I feel that I have gone mad! The police consider me dead even though I'm alive! My nephew has seized my property! I live in the guest room! My nephew says: "Indeed you do resemble my uncle but my uncle is dead; the court has accepted that he is dead, and there is no way for you to cheat me now."'

'Indeed this is a great tragedy,' Imran said in a sorrowful tone.

'It is, right?' Nawwab Hashim said. 'It means that you accept that I am Nawwab Hashim!'

'Completely, sir. Hundred per cent. Everything is possible these days! In my newspaper report I will attempt to make it clear to people that this is indeed not inconceivable.'

'Thank you, thank you. Come with me. Let's have a talk,' Nawwab Hashim said, moving inside. Imran followed him. They came to a room.

'But I am surprised, why has your nephew let you stay here?' Imran said as he sat down. 'I mean, in this case he should have stayed away from you.'

'I am surprised myself,' Nawwab Hashim said. 'His attitude towards me is not bad. He says: "You resemble my uncle to a great degree, that's why I feel affection towards you. If you like you can live with me all your life. I will always serve you, but just don't say that you are Nawwab Hashim."'

'This is very strange.' Imran shook his head. There was a moment of silence.

Then Nawwab Hashim said, 'But how will you prove that I am indeed Nawwab Hashim?'

'I will try to prove this in every possible way, sir!' Imran said. He was silent for a while, and then asked in a secretive tone, 'You must have a few old girlfriends who still live in this city, right?'

'Why! What does that have to do with anything?' Nawwab Hashim glared at him, furious.

'Oho! Just watch the fun! All you need to do is give me their addresses; I will fix the issue in an instant! Yes sir!'

'I should at least know what you are planning to do.'

'Wait! Just answer one question. Do you really want others to believe that you are indeed Nawwab Hashim?'

'You are wasting my time!' Nawwab Hashim was irritated.

'I want to tell you, Nawwab Sahib, that if you are proved to be Nawwab Hashim, the police will come after you. In fact, I think that you might have already involved yourself with the police. It is obvious that the police will trouble you about the person whose corpse was taken to be yours.'

'My God! What do I do... I wish I had known of these events beforehand; I would have never returned!'

'But now you cannot go anywhere either!' Imran said.

'I too feel the same!' Nawwab Hashim said, visibly agitated now.

'But why did you disappear in such a mysterious way?' Imran asked.

'Just stop it! Whatever happens I'll face it, I will see to it! I don't want to become the talk of the town by digging up the past. And then, why should I even talk to you about these things, son?'

'Okay, don't tell me. But I know that shortly you will be in big trouble,' Imran said, standing up. He began to walk out of the room.

'Just a second,' Nawwab Hashim said, standing up as well. 'What will you write about me?'

'That you are not Nawwab Hashim,' Imran stopped and replied, but without turning.

'I will sue your newspaper!'

'Yes, only if the court accepts that you are Nawwab Hashim,' Imran said calmly.

'You can't do that!' Nawwab Hashim shouted.

'No one can stop me!' Imran shouted back.

'I will shoot you!' Nawwab Hashim was still incensed.

'Let me see your gun,' Imran replied. 'One needs guts to kill!'

Gesticulating wildly, Imran began arguing with the Nawwab. The argument escalated rapidly and they almost came to fisticuffs. A gaggle of servants gathered outside. Then a handsome, large, well-built man entered the room. He could not have been more than thirty. He seemed quite agile despite his big frame.

'What's the matter?' he asked thunderously.

'He...he...' Nawwab Hashim said, pointing at Imran, 'is a reporter for some newspaper.'

'So! What's the point of all this ruckus?'

'He threatens to write an article against me in the newspaper!'

'Why, sir, what's the matter?' He turned towards Imran.

'You are perhaps Nawwab Sajid?'

'Yes sir! But you for no reason...'

'Wait a minute!' Imran said, raising his hand. 'I actually wanted to meet you, but this gentleman interfered. He tells me that he is Nawwab Hashim.'

'Why, sir?' He turned towards Nawwab Hashim. 'I had warned you, hadn't I, that you weren't to talk such nonsense.'

'Listen to me, Sajid, you will burn in hell for this. I am your uncle!'

'If you are my uncle then I only have one piece of advice for you: leave quietly because if you don't, the police is going to give you a lot of trouble!' Then he looked towards Imran and said, 'Right, sir?'

'Certainly, certainly!' Imran said, nodding. 'In fact, most certainly, sir!'

'Okay sir! Why did you want to meet me?'

'Aha...actually the thing is that I wanted to exchange thoughts about dogs with you.'

Nawwab Sajid stared at Imran. He was a dog lover and no one in the whole city had more dogs than him.

'It doesn't seem from your appearance that you would be interested in dogs!' Nawwab Sajid said after a while.

'There is no doubt that I still look like a human being...but I know a lot about dogs!'

'What do you know?'

'That sometimes dogs start barking without a reason!'

'Hmm! So you are from the CIB,' Nawwab Sajid said, staring at Imran.

'No, I am from the A to Z. Don't worry about it, but I would definitely like to exchange notes about dogs with you!'

'Of course, please do, sir!' Nawwab Sajid said, sitting on a chair. 'I'd like to know just one thing. Can you tell me how many breeds of hunting dogs exist? From your answer I'll be able to gauge your knowledge of dogs.'

'All breeds of dogs are extremely fond of hunting.'

'By hunters I mean sporting breeds!'

'Oh, then say that!' Imran said, nodding. 'Okay, count on your fingers...Basenji, Borzoi, Dachshund, Greyhound, Afghan Hound, Irish Wolfhound, Beagle, Harrier...Foxhound, Otterhound, Bloodhound, Deer-hound, Elkhound, Beast hound, Saluki and may God keep you alive...Whippet... Yes, so tell me—would you also like to know their habits and their social and political inclinations? I'd be happy to shed light on that as well!'

'No, that's enough. You are certainly interested in dogs. Yes, so what would you like to discuss about dogs?'

'I am actually researching extinct breeds of dogs,' Imran said.

'Extinct breeds?'

'Yes sir! So what do you know about local breeds?'

'Local breeds!' Nawwab Sajid exclaimed, wincing in disgust.

'Yes sir! Local breeds! Foreign breeds lord over local breeds even today! This is so shameful! You embrace foreign breeds and spurn local ones.'

'Oh, are you the leader of local breeds?' Nawwab Sajid said, laughing.

'Okay, let's leave it at that. As I was saying...'

'Wait! I don't know anything about local breeds,' Nawwab Sajid said, standing up. 'Surely, you must have other things you need to attend to.' He left the room, leaving Imran and Nawwab Hashim still sitting there.

They both sat in silence for a few minutes. Nawwab Hashim stared at Imran strangely. After a while he said, 'Who the hell *are* you?'

'I am Ali Imran—MSc, DSc! Officer on Special Duty from the Central Intelligence Bureau. Will you talk to me now?!'

'Oh, then indeed my nephew is very shrewd!' Nawwab Hashim said laughing. 'Wait, I'll call him!'

'Hold on. I'm done with my enquiry.'

'Friend, you would make a worthy associate...'

'I am worthy of more, Nawwab Sahib! I can claim with certainty that indeed you are Nawwab Hashim.'

'Another somersault!' Nawwab Hashim laughed loudly. Then he became serious. 'Go now or else I'll be compelled to call the police!'

'Thanks for the advice.' Imran left quietly. While crossing the garden walkway his eyes happened to fall on the disorderly begonia bushes. It seemed as if someone was hiding in them. Imran immediately began walking faster. He walked out of the gate, got into his car, and began driving.

In the rear-view mirror he saw a car come out of the haveli and head in his direction. Imran suddenly swerved into a byroad. The car was still following him. At one point the car came very close, and at that instant the constable at the roundabout signalled the traffic to a stop. The car which had been following him was now right behind his car. He turned and looked behind. Nawwab Hashim's nephew Sajid was at the wheel.

Imran moved his car forward. He stopped at another roundabout and looked behind him. Sajid's car was still there. As soon as Imran looked back Sajid waved his hand and signalled at him to stop. When the traffic started moving again, Imran drove on. He didn't seem to be in a great hurry.

A short while later Imran pulled over next to a restaurant. He stood at the door of the restaurant and watched as Nawwab Sajid got out of his car. He darted towards Imran like an arrow.

'You seem not to have heard me,' he said, smiling. 'My throat is sore from shouting!'

'It seems that you have seriously deliberated upon the abject condition of local breeds!'

'Come, let's talk inside.'

'But the topic of discussion will only be local breeds,' Imran said, entering the restaurant.

The two of them sat in an empty cabin. Imran called a waiter and ordered tea.

'I eavesdropped on your conversation,' Sajid said.

'I know that,' Imran said coldly.

'So you really *are* a CIB person!'

Imran took out his visiting card from his pocket, gave it to Sajid, and said, 'If he actually is Nawwab Hashim then you will have to wash your hands off a lot of property.'

'Just on the basis of a resemblance? That's nonsense,' Sajid said.

'Ten years ago when Nawwab Hashim's corpse was found, who was in the haveli at the time?'

'The deceased lived alone with a few servants.'

'Where were you?'

'I was studying at the time and I lived in one of the hostels of Maysur College.'

'Who supported you?'

'My late uncle! Ah! I loved him dearly and when I saw his semblance in that person my heart melted. If he stops saying that he is Nawwab Hashim, I would be happy to provide for him all my life.'

'Can you tell me why Nawwab Hashim was murdered?'

'I am not ready to concede even today that it was a murder,' Sajid said thoughtfully. 'It was a suicide, I'm hundred per cent certain of that.'

'But why?'

'Circumstances, Mr Imran. The gun was found near the corpse and a streak of gunpowder was found on the face! If it were a murder case then things wouldn't have been so. The murderer could have fired a shot from a distance. I think that he must have put the muzzle to his face and pressed the trigger himself.'

'Thank you very much,' Imran replied seriously. 'You have clarified everything, but now we will have to find out why he committed suicide.' The waiter brought their tea, and Imran waited for him to leave. Then he said, 'Can you shed some light on possible reasons for his suicide?'

'Oh! I think it was some problem related to a love affair and all of that stuff,' Nawwab Sajid said, slightly embarrassed.

'Good.' Imran rubbed his chin in thought. After a few moments he said, 'Can I have the address of his girlfriend?'

'I don't know her address.'

'Where were you on the night this incident happened?'

'In the hostel!'

'Okay. Now if it is proved that indeed this person is Nawwab Hashim, what will you do?'

'I will go mad!' Nawwab Sajid said, visibly agitated.

'Very appropriate!' Imran nodded his head seriously. At that moment he appeared to be an utter fool.

'What?' Sajid became even more agitated.

'I mean that now you should declare yourself mad and leave for a sanatorium. Return after ten years. Nawwab Hashim will be dead by then.'

'You are making fun of me!' Nawwab Sajid shot up in anger.

'No sir! But both you uncle and nephew are making a joke of the law!'

'You again referred to that man as my uncle!'

'Sit down, sir,' Imran said gently. 'Now tell me... what is the real story?'

'I don't want to talk to you.'

'Okay, fine. Forget it. Let's talk about dogs!'

Sajid sat down, but it was clear that he was quite worried.

'I would like to ask you about that dog Raygi.'

'It's that man's dog...' Nawwab Sajid said.

'What breed is it?'

'He is a crossbred Beagle! He's a lazy dog—had he been a thoroughbred, he would have been quite wonderful!'

'Did Nawwab Hashim ever keep dogs before?'

'No. He has always hated dogs.'

'Why don't you kick him out of the haveli?' Sajid did not say anything. Imran looked at him searchingly. After some time he said, 'You know what he is doing.'

'I don't know anything! But he seems to be a very mysterious person.'

'As soon as he came to town, he met a superintendent of my department and showed him his documents.'

'What kind of documents?'

'He fought with the Allies against the Nazis for two years. He, meaning Nawwab Hashim, son of Nawwab Qasim. His rank was that of a Major. I mean, who can prove that those documents were fakes? Those have an international credibility.'

'My God!' Sajid said, wide-eyed in astonishment. He was silent for a while. Then he began talking rapidly, as though in a delirium, 'Impossible...it's wrong...it's nonsense...he's a fraud...I am going to kick him out of the haveli today!'

'But what would that do? His claim still stands.'

'Then tell me—what should I do?' Sajid said helplessly. 'I made a serious mistake by letting him stay in the haveli.'

'What if you hadn't made this mistake? Would that have changed anything?'

'What should I do now?'

'Find out the circumstances of Nawwab Hashim's death.'

'I have told you before, it was an affair with a woman!'

'Who was she? Where did she live?'

'I don't know any details. My uncle wasn't married but he knew a lot of women. One of these women was highly esteemed. She lived somewhere in Alamgiri Sirai. Once, my uncle had also picked a fight with someone because of her. However, all this is hearsay. I cannot claim with certainty that any of this is true.'

'Alamgiri Sirai...' Imran mumbled to himself. 'But nothing can be deduced from this piece of information.'

'Look, there is one more thing,' Sajid said. 'But I fear you will brush it aside.'

'Does it have hair?'

'What?' Sajid stared at him in bafflement.

'The thing that you wanted to tell me about.'

A hesitant 'no' slipped from Sajid's mouth.

'Then how can I brush it aside?' Imran lowered his head and mumbled, perplexed. Then he raised his head and gently said, 'Please say frankly whatever you want. We are not paid a salary for brushing things aside!'

'Look, it is an absurd thing, that's why...but I wonder—what if it is true.'

'Even if it isn't true I am ready to listen to it,' Imran said frustratedly.

'I know a girl from Alamgiri Sirai who greatly resembles my late uncle!'

'Why are you telling me this? How is it relevant?'

'It's possible that she is my uncle's illegitimate child!'

'How old is she?'

'Not more than twenty.'

'She must have been ten at the time when he disappeared. But one doesn't kill for a woman with a ten-year-old daughter. What do you think?'

'When did I imply that he was murdered for that woman?' Sajid said. 'It is possible that it was some other woman, but I cannot be certain of that either! Look, this is my personal opinion; resemblance alone doesn't prove that she is my uncle's daughter.'

'So you must be particularly intrigued by this girl?'

'Only to the extent that my heart desires to gaze at her. But I have not talked to her and she doesn't know me either. But I can give you her address.'

'Ah,' Imran said with a smile, 'so you have been following her.'

'What do I say, sir. When I look at her, my heart is involuntarily drawn to her.'

'If your heart is really drawn to her then do give me her address...'

'She lives in Alamgiri Sirai. There is a small yellow house near the half-minaret.'

Imran put down his cup of tea. He was visibly astonished: it was the same address Moody had given him just a while ago.

'Are you sure this girl lives in that house?' he asked Sajid.

'Oh, I have seen her going there hundreds of times,' Sajid said.

'Okay, mister. I will try...' Imran stood up without completing his sentence. He had already paid the bill.

'If I want to meet you some time, where can I find you?' Sajid asked.

'My address and phone number are on my card,' Imran replied and left the restaurant. Instead of going to his car he headed to a medical store. There, he bought a bottle of cholera medicine. The chemist not only recognized him but also seemed to know him very well; when Imran asked for a hypodermic syringe, he gave him one for free. Imran also bought a couple of ampoules of some medicine.

Chapter 5

IMRAN DROVE TO ALAMGIRI Sirai and stopped near the half-minaret. The place was mostly in ruins and so the search for a small yellow house was not too difficult. Most of the buildings in the vicinity were very old. A few, which still had their walls and ceilings intact, were inhabited, while the more derelict ones had been abandoned.

Imran stopped before the yellow house. He had left his car a distance away. He knocked on the door, but there was no response for a long time. Finally a beautiful young girl opened the door. Her lustrous large eyes were filled with fear. It also seemed that she had been crying a short while ago.

'I am a doctor,' Imran said gently. 'I've come to vaccinate you for cholera.'

The girl opened the door fully and stepped out.

'Are you a municipality doctor?' she asked. Imran could not help but notice that her voice was quavering.

'Yes indeed. You understood correctly,' Imran said. He had just seen the man who claimed to be Nawwab Hashim, and indeed there did seem to be some resemblance between him and this girl.

'I don't understand,' the girl replied timidly. 'I have lived here for the past twenty years, but I have never even heard of a government doctor visiting the area.'

'Well, the doctors are supposed to make rounds,' Imran said with a smile, 'but if a certain doctor doesn't come then that's his business. I myself have only just arrived here.'

'Will you wait for a while?' the girl asked.

'Why?'

'Actually I would also like one of my relatives to get this vaccine.'

'Oh! Don't worry about that, I will give this vaccine to everyone in this area within a week.'

'No, I beg you to do that today. I shall be very grateful to you. This man is very paranoid that he will catch cholera one of these days, especially since it's so widespread.'

'Give me his address.'

'I will fetch him...' the girl said and quickly walked into an alley, leaving Imran standing there. He felt like a fool. Five minutes later the girl still hadn't come back. Imran knocked on the door again. He expected that someone would answer the door. But despite knocking repeatedly no one answered. Five more minutes passed and now Imran began to wonder if the girl had pulled wool over his eyes and escaped... She fit Moody's description hundred per cent. Imran thought that if she had in fact tricked him, she was indeed the wiliest girl he knew. Suddenly he heard the sound of heavy footsteps approaching him. Three uniformed policemen emerged out of the alley. One of these was a sub-inspector and two were constables. The girl was with them.

They approached Imran. The girl looked at him and said, 'Kindly ask him where he has come from!'

The sub-inspector gave Imran a piercing stare. Perhaps he did not know him. 'So what kind of doctor are you?' he asked Imran.

'Doctor?' Imran said, astonished. 'Who said that I am a doctor?'

'You see, officer!' the girl said to the sub-inspector. She seemed utterly delighted.

'Then why did you pretend to be a doctor?' the sub-inspector asked heatedly.

'I never said that!' Imran said. He pointed to the girl. 'I merely asked her for Sadruddin Allahwala's address. She said, wait I'll call him. But you don't seem to be Mr Sadruddin Allahwala!'

'This is a lie, a complete lie!' the girl shouted, agitated.

'Oh God, forgive me!' Imran said, holding his ears. 'Don't you dare call me a liar.'

'No, mister. These histrionics won't work now,' the sub-inspector said, frowning.

'So, pray, tell me which histrionics would work?' Imran shrugged his shoulders.

'You will have to come to the police station with me.' The sub-inspector was now seething with anger.

'Could you come to the side for a minute, please,' Imran said. He took the sub-inspector to a corner of the alley at a considerable distance from the girl and the constables. However, both the parties could still easily see each other. Imran removed his card from his pocket and handed it to the sub-inspector. On reading the card, the sub-inspector first looked at Imran with amazement. He then took three steps back and saluted Imran. The girl and both the constables observed this performance in shock. The sub-inspector was now stammering, 'Ex-excuse me…I wasn't familiar with you, but sir, this girl is very worried.'

'Why?'

'She claims that someone stole twenty-five thousand rupees from her house and also that some strangers have been after her for a while.'

'Hmm… Who else is in that house?'

'No one. She lives alone. Her father died a month ago.'

'Didn't you ask where she got this money? She doesn't seem affluent enough to have twenty-five thousand rupees in cash lying around the house.'

'Yes indeed. I understand. But the girl seems to be from a good family.'

'A good family?' Imran repeated in surprise. Then he said, assuming a severe tone, 'Kindly do not make the department a grocery shop. A good family is only under consideration when one has to give credit. Now, please leave. Actually no, wait. Have you filed a formal theft report?'

The sub-inspector looked baffled. 'Sir, actually the thing is that...'

'The girl is pretty, as well as young!' Imran completed the sentence. 'If you haven't filed a report then why did you come with her so eagerly?'

'Sir, actually...'

'Go away!' Imran roared.

The sub-inspector swallowed hard. The girl and the constables had also heard Imran roar. The sub-inspector left quietly. When the constables saw this they slipped away as well. The girl remained where she was. Imran approached her.

'Is your name Durdana?'

'Yes.'

'Did you sell a jewellery box to Mr Walter Moody?'

'Yes indeed,' the girl said. There was no hesitation in her voice.

'Was it yours?'

'But why should I tell you anything?'

'Because an officer from the Investigation Bureau is asking you these questions.'

The girl looked at him silently for a while and then said, 'Yes, it was mine indeed. My mother inherited it. Some mysterious men wanted to steal it from me. That's why I sold it to Mr Moody.'

'For twenty-five thousand!'

'Yes! And now those twenty-five thousand are gone!' The girl was visibly distressed.

'How did that happen?'

'Thieves stole the money! I think it must be the same mysterious people who have been eyeing the jewellery box for a long time. They also hovered around Mr Moody but their efforts proved to be unfruitful.'

'The matter indeed has borne fruit now!' Imran said, nodding.

'I don't understand!'

'The bedbugs and mosquitoes in a police lock-up make one understand everything.'

'But what do I have to do with a police lock-up?'

'Look girl, this pretence won't work. Just tell me the whereabouts of your aides. You can even save yourself by confessing that you were merely an instrument in their plan and were not aware of the gravity of the situation.'

'I don't know what you are talking about, sir!'

'Even a hundred and fifty rupees would be too much for the jewellery box which you sold for twenty-five thousand!'

'You must have misjudged its worth,' she said smiling. 'It is studded with stones worth thousands.'

'Those are counterfeits! Imitations!'

'Impossible. I can't believe that.'

Imran scrutinized her. A while later he asked, 'Do you know Nawwab Hashim?'

'I don't know him.'

'Nawwab Sajid?'

'What do you want? Why would I know any nawwabs? Do you think I fraternize with aristocrats?'

'No, I wasn't implying that. So, yes, we were talking about that jewellery box.'

'But what makes you think those jewels are fake?'

'Don't embroil me in a pointless debate. Tell me the names of your aides.'

'My God!' the girl said, holding her head with both hands and leaning against the wall. 'I seem to be in deep trouble!'

'I am telling you the truth. As long as you confess you won't be in any trouble. Now come on, tell me the names of your aides.'

'I swear by God I don't have any aides! I am completely friendless.'

'Okay, girl,' Imran said, drawing a deep breath. 'Do you belong to a royal family?'

'I don't know... However, that's what I...'

'Was told, right? Good!' Imran said quickly. 'Who told you?'

'A well-wisher of mine.'

'Aha! I mean I want the address of that very well-wisher.'

'I don't know his address.'

'Girl, don't waste my time!'

'I swear by God! I don't know his address. Since my father's death he has helped me a lot. Perhaps he is one of my father's close friends.'

'And you don't know his address? That's surprising.'

'No, don't be surprised. I came to know that he was my father's friend after my father's death.'

'When did your father die?'

'About a month ago. I wasn't even here. I was out of town for some important work. Father fell really ill at that time. It's possible that he might have called his friend to look after him. Anyway, when I returned he had been dead two days and I only saw his grave... The neighbours informed me that his last rites were performed with great splendour. I was already aware of the existence of this jewellery box and I always thought it was very valuable—even in the course of my father's life some mysterious men had tried to steal it.'

'What advice did your father's friend give you?'

'That I should get this jewellery box to a safe place. I asked him to keep it with him but he said that he would be in danger too. He said: "If some foreigner, meaning an Englishman or an American, can help you, that would be the best." He suggested Moody Sahib who has often been seen in this area.'

'Moody has been seen in this area?!'

'Yes, of course! Often. I have seen him several times. Yes, so one day my father's friend was also here. Coincidentally Moody Sahib's car passed by our house and he suggested that I take the jewellery box and get in the car. The car was moving slowly. I got in and did whatever he had instructed me to do, that is, tell him that I belong to a royal family. I'm sure Moody Sahib has told you the rest. What more can I tell you? My head is spinning.'

'So you don't belong to a royal family?'

'I don't know what family I belong to. My father never told me. He was a very learned man. You will find piles and piles of books at our place.'

'Okay, what did he do?'

'He used to make daguerreotype photographs. It brought in a lot of money. But he hasn't done anything for the past six years, ever since he returned from his four-year absence.'

'I don't understand.'

'You have been standing here for quite a while. Do come inside,' the girl said. 'If the gems of the jewellery box are indeed fake then I will be compelled to commit suicide, because Moody Sahib's money has also been stolen.'

They both came in. There were cupboards full of books on all four walls of the room which they entered.

'This is a long story, sir...' The girl had barely begun talking when someone knocked on the door. 'Just a minute,' the girl said. She got up and went to answer the door. Imran began examining the room carefully. Suddenly he heard a voice and was taken aback—it was Moody's voice. The next moment the girl entered the room with Moody.

'Imran!' Moody halted at the door in surprise.

'Come, come,' Imran said, smiling.

'What did you do! I hope you haven't said anything untoward to Her Ladyship.'

'Shut up. Come here and sit quietly.'

'No! I don't like this. I don't care about my money. You should leave this place. Whatever Her Ladyship did was fine. I don't have any complaints.'

'You fool! If you babble nonsense I will get you locked up as well!' Imran said. Moody sneered.

'Are some clothes burning somewhere?' Imran asked, looking at the girl.

'I too smell something similar,' the girl replied.

Moody started babbling again. Imran continued to think, paying him no attention. Suddenly a thick cloud of smoke entered the room and all three of them shot up from their seats in shock. Imran jumped to a window. Clouds of smoke were welling up from a room.

'Fire!' the girl cried and ran towards that room. Both the men also rushed in behind her. A big pile of clothes and documents was burning in the middle of the room. It appeared as though these things had been gathered together and deliberately set on fire.

The girl stood with her hands crossed on her chest as if she were a priestess from some ancient Temple of Fire. Her eyes were wide in horror and her lips quivered with fear. Suddenly she slid to the floor in a faint.

Chapter 6

IMRAN PACED ABOUT THE room as Captain Fayyaz stared at him murderously. 'Look, Fayyaz,' Imran stopped pacing up and down and said, 'This case is very complicated. Whether Nawwab Hashim was murdered or whether he committed suicide, both situations are equally ridiculous. After all, why did the murderer fire at his face? The chest or the forehead is a more appropriate target. Death occurs almost immediately in that case... I have studied the file meticulously. There was not a single scratch anywhere on the dead man's body except on his face. And where was the corpse? On the bed! The deceased was lying flat on his back. Fayyaz, I ask you, what evidence do you have that the blood on the bed was the dead man's blood?'

'I don't have the energy to listen to your nonsense. A few minutes ago you were telling me the story of a girl who had sold Moody a jewellery box. Now you have jumped to Nawwab Hashim's murder.'

'You answer my question.'

'The blood on the bed was not the blood of the person who died?' Fayyaz said with a laugh. Then he said seriously, 'You are a responsible man now. Give up this amateur speculation.'

'Fayyaz Sahib, I am even ready to state that the death did not occur in that room! I think he was killed by strangulation elsewhere. Then the visage was disfigured by firing a shot at the face.

'Since the culprit wanted the gunshot to be understood as the cause of the death, he put the corpse on the bed, and after soaking the bed with some other blood, he fled. If this is not true then why were there no traces of resistance in the room, tell me?'

'Resistance? Come on, what are you talking about! Son, the bullet was fired while he was asleep.'

'So this means that ten years ago your Bureau was an orphanage, the supreme house of mismanagement.'

'Why?'

'Because Captain Sahib, the report in the file is completely incomplete!'

'Why? Why is it incomplete?'

'Friend! You are indeed the manager of an orphanage—your mismanagement is exemplary. I think that even your attendant could have managed things better than you have.'

'Please, will you talk some sense now?' Fayyaz was enraged.

'You too admit that the gunshot was fired at close quarters. This suggests that the distance between the mouth of the gun and the face was less than six inches.'

'This fact has been repeated to death.'

'Okay then, Fayyaz Sahib, why was no pellet found in the bed? Or why were there no traces of gunpowder on the bed?'

'There must have been some.'

'But, my lord, there is no mention of this in the report. This incident is a mere ten years old, not a hundred years old. You can't get away by making excuses that there was no knowledge of forensics. I contend that the investigator did not find any traces of gunpowder near the face, otherwise he would have definitely mentioned it. And then give me that file which contains the report of the chemical analysis of the blood.'

'We didn't think it necessary to investigate the blood type. All of us were agreed that it was the blood of the deceased.'

'When people start losing courage they readily agree to claims like this. You people always shy away from complications. You iron out complexities with such dexterity that one is amazed. The post-mortem report clearly states that the death occurred because of sudden heart failure and you guys are obsessed with the gunshot.'

'Yes, that's completely true,' said Fayyaz, nodding. 'He was sleeping when suddenly there was a blast near his ear and his heart failed. That was why he didn't even have a chance to writhe in pain, and so the bed was not creased. His body turned cold in the same position.'

'My objection is still valid. Why were there no pellets in the bed after all? What became of them? Did the gun's heart also fail at that moment?'

'To hell with it,' Fayyaz said irritably. 'The case rests with you. Go! Do whatever you want, I am least concerned. But yes, you were talking about that girl, that case seems really interesting. So then what did you do when she fainted?'

'Kept my shirt on and kept beating my head for quite some time.' Imran slid his hand into his pocket, looking for a packet of chewing gum.

'What caused the fire?'

'I am sure it was a match or a cigar or a lighter.'

'You are strange,' Fayyaz said, annoyed.

Imran didn't say anything. After a few minutes of silence, he said, 'The girl is creating a new problem for me.'

'Oh, so do you think she is actually innocent?'

'Can't say anything at the moment because I haven't been able to find out all the details, and the girl has been admitted to the hospital. I am going there right now.'

Chapter 7

MOODY HAD ADMITTED THE girl to a private room in Central Hospital. He stayed the night with her, preoccupied with his dreams of the girl's royal lineage. The girl attempted to convince him that she had sold him the jewellery box because she thought that the gems were genuine. But Moody prevented her from talking, telling her that it was stressful and would affect her health.

At this moment, Moody was sitting reverently beside her bed and staring at the floor.

'Moody Sahib, I am quite well now,' the girl said.

'I am grateful to the heavens! Grateful to those tall mountains...and grateful to the ancient rivers which have seen the grandeur and glory of kings of yore. Your Royal Highness, congratulations on regaining your health.'

'Don't mock me. I am already very embarrassed. If those gems are fake, I'll try to return your money by any means possible. I will sell my father's library. It must be worth twenty-five thousand rupees! I remember clearly that once someone offered to buy a manuscript for twenty-five hundred rupees but father declined to sell it... And please don't address me as

Your Ladyship. I am not a princess. I told you that I was from a royal family because someone told me to do so.'

'You are a princess! Don't break my heart, tell me that you are a princess. Command me to spread the wealth of the world at your feet. Think of me as one of the slaves of your forefathers, who would willingly spill his blood at the behest of his masters.'

The girl looked at him in astonishment; Moody seemed quite sincere.

'Is Imran Sahib your friend?'

'Yes, of course. He is my friend. You don't need to worry at all. I will protect you with a wall of money... and of course I won't lodge a complaint against you, so you have nothing to fear. The police won't be able to harm you in any way whatsoever.'

There was a soft knock on the door and the next moment Imran entered the room. He looked a bit foolish, as always. It seemed as though he had entered the wrong room, and he would apologize for his mistake, turn around, and leave.

'Are you feeling better now?'

'Yes, I am. I am fine now.'

'But you will not say anything that might upset her, do you understand!' Moody said to Imran.

'Yes, I do.' Imran blinked his eyes rapidly. Then he said to the girl, 'Could you kindly describe the appearance of your father's friend to me?'

'Appearance? I can't say anything, except that he has a thick beard and that he wears dark glasses because he has some eye problem.'

'Hmm.' Imran shrugged his shoulders. But it was difficult to say how the girl's words affected him. He then asked, 'Where were you when your father died?'

'I wasn't here... I lost all my senses when I heard about his death on my return... His funeral arrangements were taken care of by the same person who has been claiming to be his friend.'

'That's fine. But didn't your neighbours tell you anything peculiar about it?'

'Peculiar? I don't understand what you mean.'

'Where was the corpse given the last bath?'

'Oh...yes...some relatives of father took him from our house. And perhaps the last bath and shrouding were performed at some friend's place.'

'However, no neighbour could see the face of the deceased.'

'What are you implying?' The girl adjusted herself and sat up attentively. They were talking in Urdu. Moody tried to say something but Imran signalled him to stop.

'Oh yes,' Imran interrupted without answering the girl's question, 'you mentioned an incident that occurred ten years ago?'

'Are you talking about father's disappearance?' The girl said this in English. Perhaps she wanted to make Moody aware of her circumstances. Imran nodded.

The girl remained silent for a while and then said, 'Father was a very mysterious person. I haven't been able to understand what he was, or who he was, until now. When I was ten years old, he suddenly disappeared. I was left all alone. My mother had died at the time of my birth. Just imagine my condition! I didn't even know if Father had any relatives whom I could contact. He had never mentioned any. Anyway, it was very taxing... There was a poor Christian family that lived in the neighbourhood. They helped me a lot—got me admitted into a mission school and took care of me in every way possible. I will never forget Mrs Hardy. What a great woman! She looked after me like a mother! She even bore all my expenses, and never once insisted that I convert to Christianity.'

The girl was silent for a while. Then she said, 'There was no news of Father for four years. Then suddenly he returned one day. He kept crying for weeks, but didn't tell me anything about where he had been all this time. But he said that he would never leave me again.'

'Did he never go anywhere then?' Imran asked.

'No. He rarely ever left the house. Before his disappearance he used to make daguerreotypes for a living. After returning he gave that up as well. But until today I haven't been able find out how he earned his money. He didn't seem to do any work. But we were never short of money.'

'And perhaps he brought that jewellery box back with him?' Imran asked.

'No! I have seen it since my childhood.'

'Okay! But when did those suspicious men start coming for it?'

'Only after Father's death. Before that, no one had ever come for it.'

Imran thought for a while. Then he said, 'Were there any regular visitors during the past six years?'

'No one. Even close neighbours didn't like to talk to Father.'

'But why? Was he such a grouch?'

'Not at all. He was very well mannered and sociable. He never spoke to anyone harshly. I think that people thought badly of him only because he had abandoned me.'

'But where did all these friends emerge from on his death?' Imran asked.

'I myself was surprised. I found out from my neighbours that there were five of them. But only one of them has appeared before me...the same one who told me what to do about the jewellery box.'

'And he has not been seen after that?'

'No, he met me even after that, but it was only until I sold the jewellery box!'

'Did your father ever even mention a friend?'

'He mentioned only one friend, the one whom I had gone to see just a few days before his death.'

'His name and address?' Imran said, removing a diary from his pocket.

'Hakim Moinuddin, 47 Faridabad, Dilawarpur.'

'Why did you go to see him?'

'Father had sent me,' the girl said. 'Father had a liver problem. His pain was greatly aggravated during those days. His treatment continued, but to no advantage. Ultimately he asked me to go to Moinuddin Sahib. Perhaps Hakim Sahib had a tried prescription for this problem. I went to Dilawarpur. But the medicine was not ready. That's why I had to stay there for four days. I informed my father through a telegram. He telegrammed me back saying that I should not return without the medicine, even if it took me ten days.'

'Can we still find Hakim Sahib there?' Imran asked.

'Why not? Of course.'

'But what if we are unable to find him?'

'What can I say about that?' the girl replied, rubbing her forehead anxiously. 'I don't understand. What is going on after all?'

'Enough Imran, stop it,' Moody interrupted, raising his hand. 'I've got to the bottom of the matter.'

'What have you understood?' the girl asked with a start.

'That your father is alive,' Moody said slowly. 'That's it. I've got it.'

'Shut up!' Imran said, frowning at him. 'I think you have a hangover. Go and get yourself a peg or two.'

'No, I am perfectly fine,' Moody said, yawning.

Imran asked the girl, 'Could you provide me a photograph of your father?'

'Sadly, no. The things that were burnt mysteriously also contained his photo albums. Or perhaps his albums were not in that pile… I don't know, I'm not in my senses… It's possible that I may find one upon searching… But please tell me—how long do I have to stay here? I'm completely fine now.'

'You are safer here,' Imran said, nodding. 'You are not leaving this place until I tell you that you can. I have arranged for everything—you can stay here for a while without any problems.'

'But why?'

'It's not necessary to tell you right now.'

'Imran, I am going to behead you!' Moody said threateningly. 'You are insulting Her Ladyship.'

'And what are you doing here? Get up and come with me.'

'I will stay here.'

'Shut up. Stand up. Stand!'

Chapter 8

MOODY RETURNED TO HIS house with Imran in tow. As soon as they reached his place he began pouring himself one drink after another, downing them without a pause. Good heavens! He hadn't had a drop since last night.

After two or three pegs he turned to Imran. 'What do you think of me, huh? I know everything! I have got to the bottom of the matter. Her father is alive and he seems to be a very mysterious man.'

'Stop talking nonsense. Listen to what I am saying.'

'I will not listen to anything. I have a theory.'

Imran fell silent. Moody kept blabbering. 'I am Sherlock Holmes.'

'Moody kay bacche!' Imran frowned at him.

'No, Dr Watson, you cannot understand these things,' Moody muttered as he started pacing about. Meanwhile a servant brought his pipe. Imran leaned against the back of a sofa, lost in thought. Moody lit his pipe and, raising his head in a self-satisfied way, turned to Imran. 'He knows of some royal treasure and I think he has the map to get to it too.'

Imran didn't move; his eyes were still closed. Moody remained silent for a while. Then he began,

'Ten years ago, some dangerous men must have begun following him. That's it; he disappeared, returned four years later, lived peacefully for the next six years, and then again the same or some other men began stalking him! This time he enacted his death. What say? Ha ha! Didn't understand? You guys use your stomachs instead of your brains! And now listen to the story of that jewellery box. Perhaps it belongs to the same royal treasure. His father, for the purpose of showing it to his enemies that...oh... showing what...huh...showing what!'

Moody slapped his head and was silent for a while, thinking. Then he shook Imran and said, 'What was I saying just now?'

Imran opened his eyes with a start. 'What's the matter?' he asked, agitated.

'What was I saying?' Moody hit his head again several times.

'You!' Imran shot up and frowned at him. Then he grabbed his collar, pushed him onto a sofa, and said, 'Go to hell!' And the next moment Imran was out.

Chapter 9

ABOUT A WEEK HAD passed since Nawwab Hashim's return. News of this incredible incident had spread like wildfire in the city and had also attracted attention in the whole country—it was the only hullabaloo of its kind. The Intelligence Bureau officials had not been able to find a way to resolve this matter. Currently, they had only one question in mind—if indeed this was Nawwab Hashim, then who was the person whose corpse was found in Nawwab Hashim's bedroom? Captain Fayyaz found Imran very busy these days. But it was not easy to get any information from him: he always answered every question, but his answers were so befuddling that the inquirer wanted to beat his head in frustration, but couldn't do so for fear of being tagged as a clown.

Fayyaz tried a million times but could not get any information out of Imran. However, he did get to listen to cooked-up couplets whose first verse was generally by Mirza Ghalib and the second by Dr Iqbal. For example,

The mad heart of Ghalib is a talisman of serpentine convolution,
That fleet footed, that pride of the royal stable.

Imran was an expert in making such nonsensical connections and relationships. Anyway, Fayyaz couldn't extract any information from him. Today he had summoned Nawwab Hashim and his nephew Nawwab Sajid to his office. Both had come. But both looked extremely frustrated with each other.

'Look, sir,' Fayyaz addressed Nawwab Hashim. 'Now there is just one option left.'

'What is that? Look, sir, whatever the option is, I want to get this over with as soon as possible,' Nawwab Hashim replied.

'The option is that I get you sent to jail.'

'Really?' Nawwab Hashim frowned. At this point, Imran entered the room. His hair was unkempt and his clothes were rumpled. He looked as though he had arrived from a long journey. He smiled when he saw both uncle and nephew, winked at Fayyaz, and started scratching his head.

'It will not be easy to get me sent to jail, Mr Fayyaz. After all, on what basis will you get me sent to jail?' Nawwab Hashim said, looking squarely at Fayyaz.

'There are two reasons. Whichever one you like,' Fayyaz said. 'If the deceased was indeed Nawwab Hashim, then you are an impostor; and if he was not Nawwab Hashim, then you are his murderer.'

'How am *I* the murderer?'

'The morning following the night you claim to have left, a corpse was found in your bedroom. I ask you: why did you leave so secretively?'

'I think I will have to recount that matter now!' Nawwab Hashim had an embarrassed smile on his face.

'Recount, sir,' Imran said, taking a deep breath. 'Your situation has perplexed me!'

Nawwab Hashim turned around with a start. Perhaps he had not noticed Imran's presence. 'Oh... you...so do you belong to the Bureau?'

'You were about to say something.' Fayyaz turned Nawwab Hashim's attention back to him.

'Yes, of course. Now I will have to narrate that matter. Today, I think of it as such an ordinary matter. But at that time, it was as though a madness had taken over me! Only if I had endured that blow, and hadn't cared about what people say, I wouldn't have been in this situation today! Anyway, now listen, sir. But no, first tell me one thing...'

'Look, don't stretch the matter unnecessarily. We don't have time for nonsense!' Fayyaz said, lighting a cigarette.

'No, I'll keep it short. Okay, let me tell you frankly. I was madly in love with a woman. Apparently, she loved me too. Another aristocrat of the city was also in love with her. And so the tension between us had made this matter famous in the whole city. Apparently the woman liked me more than the other man. This was also common knowledge. But in all this uncertainty... God knows what happened but in the meantime that wretched woman ran away with a coachman. Just think about it! What would you have felt if you were in my place! Wouldn't you have wanted to hide away in a place where you would have no chance of coming across any of your acquaintances? To avoid the humiliation of the situation I thought it best to leave without telling anyone anything. But on the eve of the day I had planned to leave, one of my friends arrived from abroad. He was my closest friend. But to tell you the truth, even *his* presence was heavy on my heart that day.' Nawwab Hashim paused and lit a cigarette, took a few puffs, and then continued. 'He wasn't aware of the circumstances. I decided that I should leave before he finds out. So I did. I went away leaving him asleep.'

'So then that was your friend's body?' Fayyaz leaned forward and asked.

'Of course, it must be his body. Look, what do I tell you—I think my arch enemy and rival in love, whom I just told you about, could well have done that! Of course he must have had to face a lot of humiliation about his girlfriend's running away with the coachman, and he must have thought that I made her do that just to dupe him. So he probably resolved to avenge himself and murdered my friend Sajjad, mistaking him for me.'

'But then again, I think that it is not possible,' Nawwab Hashim added.

'But who was your rival, after all? Tell me his name,' Fayyaz said.

'Mirza Naseer.'

'Oh, the one who lived in the first bungalow, the yellow house on your street?' Imran said.

'Yes indeed, it is him.' Nawwab Hashim replied.

'It's very sad to hear that,' Imran said gloomily. 'He died last year. Now whom should I arrest? Will his son do?' Fayyaz frowned at Imran. But Imran sighed deeply. He started shaking his head, his eyes fixed on the floor.

'But I am not sure if Mirza Naseer would have done this,' Nawwab Hashim said. 'If he did that, then why did he need to make the face unidentifiable? Okay, let's assume that he killed him mistakenly. But he would have never disfigured the face. Now you yourself can guess who the culprit is!'

'Other than your nephew, who could it be, Uncle,' Imran murmured.

'What do you mean?' Sajid shot up from his seat.

'Please sit down!' Fayyaz said harshly.

'You have really got to the bottom of the matter,' Nawwab Hashim said, looking at Imran.

'I got it, right? Haha!' Imran laughed absurdly.

'Enough!' Sajid said to Nawwab Hashim threateningly. 'Your foul play is not going to work!'

'Don't get angry, my son,' Nawwab Hashim said sarcastically. 'A son can murder his father for money, you are just a nephew. And then you didn't have a penny to your name! Your father had already squandered his inheritance. And I was a bachelor. Of course, you would have been declared my heir. Am I saying anything incorrect?'

'This is nonsense. Hundred per cent nonsense. You are not Nawwab Hashim. Your documents are all fake!'

'And perhaps even my face is fake! So fake that you allowed me to stay in the haveli!'

'You cannot blame me for a murder!' Sajid said, punching the table.

'Look, mister,' Fayyaz said roughly, 'this is not your haveli but my office. Kindly keep your limbs under control!'

'Oh...please excuse me,' Sajid murmured. Then he turned to Nawwab Hashim and said, 'Let's see how your eloquence helps you in court!'

'Yes, so Captain Sahib, as I was saying,' Nawwab Hashim started speaking without paying heed, 'my nephew saw that it was a good time: if Hashim was murdered that day then it would all be on Mirza Naseer's head. He entered the haveli like a thief the same night and murdered Sajjad, mistaking him for me. I am sure he must have realized his mistake immediately, and that's why he made the body unidentifiable... He must have searched for me first, but when he didn't find me he defaced the deceased... And then, sir, tell me this: who identified the corpse?'

'Indeed your illustrious nephew here,' Fayyaz said, looking at Sajid.

'Just think about it. He is my nephew. The corpse's face was disfigured. On what basis did he declare it my body, after all? Because the deceased had my clothes on his body!'

Fayyaz didn't say anything. His eyes were fixed on Sajid's face. Imran, on the other hand, was staring at Nawwab Hashim intently.

'Answer me, Captain Sahib,' Nawwab Hashim said to Fayyaz.

'Why sir, on what basis did you declare it to be Nawwab Hashim's body?' Fayyaz asked Sajid.

'I recognized his hands and feet!' Sajid said, wiping the sweat from his brow. He looked anxious.

'Yes, yes, why not. You had already disfigured the face and disfigured it to such an extent that your identification would seal the matter! Of course, in light of this flimsy identification the police could have been satisfied only by your statement, because you were my only family member.'

Sajid did not say anything. He was glaring at Nawwab Hashim as though he would strangle him at the first opportunity.

'Yes, Mr Sajid, what do you say in your defence?' Fayyaz said sternly.

'Well, now I will answer any questions only in the presence of my lawyer,' Sajid replied.

'That's all we need!' Nawwab Hashim said sarcastically.

'I am not talking to you. And yes, now you can't return with me to the haveli! Do you understand! If you even try to come close then *you* will be responsible for the consequences!'

'No, this is not possible,' Imran interrupted. 'Why don't you two come to a compromise? And live together in that bungalow peacefully. I am sorry that I don't have an uncle or a nephew. Otherwise I would have shown you how an uncle and a nephew are one life and two bolts...no, one life two olds... Huh? What nonsense am I uttering, Super Fayyaz... What's that idiom...one life...two bolts...ch ch ch... Ahan! Moulds, moulds...one life and two moulds...wow...hunh!' As always, Imran had started talking nonsense.

'But what will their compromise achieve?' Fayyaz interrupted, ignoring Imran's mutterings. 'That corpse is going to be a bone of contention anyway.'

'Come now, leave it already,' Imran said seriously. 'How unfair that a mere corpse has become a reason for conflict between an uncle and his nephew. After all, of what use is that corpse to them!'

'Okay, kindly get out now,' Fayyaz said coldly, making a face.

But this did not affect Imran in the least. He said with a smile, 'I can prove that this murder is related to Mirza Naseer. Why, Fayyaz Sahib? What Nawwab Hashim is thinking about his nephew, wouldn't that have occurred to Mirza Naseer too?'

'What?'

'That defacing the corpse would make everyone doubt Sajid.'

'What a wonderful point!' Sajid jumped up, excited. He turned to Fayyaz and said, 'Now what do you have to say to this?'

'Oh, let it go!' Imran said, raising his hand. 'Just leave it. But both of you will live in the haveli. For no other reason but this: that my men are not troubled.'

'I don't understand,' Nawwab Hashim said.

'My men have been watching both of you. If either of you go somewhere else, I will have to increase the number of my men.'

Fayyaz frowned at Imran. Perhaps he was thinking that Imran should not have mentioned that the two men were under surveillance. Their jaws dropping in astonishment, Sajid and Nawwab Hashim were staring at Imran.

'Now both of you should leave,' Imran said to them. 'Whichever one of you abandons the haveli will be under arrest.'

'I don't understand. What are you talking about?' Sajid said.

'Attendant!' Imran cried like a beggar in the street, hitting the bell on the table.

'Okay...okay...fine,' Nawwab Hashim said, raising his hand. 'I will not leave the haveli. But you will be responsible for protecting me.'

'Don't worry. I am willing to shoulder that responsibility until you rest in your grave,' Imran said gravely.

The two men left.

Fayyaz stared at Imran. 'You are a complete ass,' he said.

'No. I belong to a different branch, we don't have superintendents there!'

'Why did you tell them that they are being watched? Now they will be alert. You do some really stupid things sometimes while trying to act like a fool.'

'Ah, Captain Fayyaz! That's why the madness of youth is so notorious,' Imran said yet another phrase that went over Fayyaz's head. Then, turning on his heel, he left the room.

One of his subordinates, designated to watch over the girl's house, had informed Imran that he had seen some suspicious people around the house during the day. Imran left his car on the main road and walked to the yellow house. As he approached the house he saw a dark human shadow at the corner of the street. Imran stopped. He sensed that the shadow was trying to hide.

'Hoopoe,' Imran said softly.

'Ye-yes, Yo-Your Honour,' came a cry. Imran had named this subordinate of his Hoopoe. He stammered while speaking. And for some reason, sight of him brought a hoopoe to mind. When Imran had called him Hoopoe for the very first time, he had been extremely displeased. He told Imran that he was of noble birth from both his mother's and father's sides, that he belonged to a family of high rank, and that he would not tolerate this insult. Imran tried to explain to him that people in the Bureau should actually have such names for security reasons. However, the man agreed to the alias Hoopoe only after much difficulty. There was another peculiar thing about Hoopoe, which was very funny given his appearance: he always tried to use very abstruse words, and on top of it, he stammered—it seemed as though he was perpetually under an attack of hysteria.

'What's the news?' Imran asked him.

He came close to Imran. 'Un-until now, no-nothing has come to pass,' Hoopoe said.

'But when did I enquire about a pass?' Imran asked confusedly. God alone knew whether he had not heard correctly or he was doing this intentionally.

'Ye-yes. You-Your Honour...I-I-I mean that... ye-yes...nuh-no change has taken place in the circumstances...o-or in other words...fa-from then until now...i-it's...e-ex-exact-exactly...a-as it was... be-before.'

'Come with me.'

'Wi-with my heart and soul, I but follow you...'

Both of them advanced to the house. There was a death-like silence in the colony. Sounds of children crying occasionally punctuated the air, but then all went silent again. Perhaps the dogs of this colony were also stoned. Imran was very surprised that he hadn't heard any dogs barking. Initially he had thought that it would be impossible to even step into the colony at this time because of the dogs.

They had only walked for a short distance when Imran almost fell, stumbling over something. Something soft and squishy. Imran bent down quickly and examined it. It was a dog's carcass.

'Wh-what came to pass, sir?' Hoopoe asked.

'Nothing came, only passed. Now come,' Imran replied. When they reached the house both of them stood hugging the wall. Since it was very dark there was no chance of them being spotted even from a very short distance.

'Sis...sis,' Hoopoe was about to whisper when Imran pressed his shoulder. He could see something moving at a short distance. It seemed as though some quadruped was approaching them slowly. Then lo and behold the number of these quadrupeds increased. One, two, three...four...five! Imran's right hand was in his coat pocket and he tightly squeezed the butt of his revolver. As soon as they reached the wall the quadrupeds stood upright. Imran had already guessed it—they were five men but couldn't be recognized as humans because it was absolutely dark. Imran put his hand on Hoopoe's chest, in an attempt to restrain him from doing something stupid.

'Arrr...hush!' Hoopoe jumped, jerking Imran's hand.

The five men also started and then ran. Imran leaped and got hold of one. 'Stop! Or I will shoot you,' he called out to the rest. But to no avail. They had already disappeared into the darkness. The man in Imran's grip was struggling to get away.

'Oh, you son of a...!' Imran shouted at Hoopoe.

'Luh-luh-look, sir.' Hoopoe was now trembling. 'I-I...am fuh-fuh-from a noble family...first Hoopoe, now son of a...wow...that's some courage, sir...I...'

'Shut up. Turn on the torch.'

'It fe-fell somewhere.'

Meanwhile Imran punched his quarry's face a few times and the man fell flat.

'Come here,' he called Hoopoe again. 'Open the knot of his tie.'

Hoopoe began examining Imran's neck in confusion.

'You ass...this is me!'

'What do you mean...*you ass*?! What untoward language for a puh-puh-person of no-no-noble birth. ...I am not some lowly grocer or butcher... Un-

un-unencumber me…right now…from this vocation… ye-yes…nuh-now.'

'Move, or I'll wring your neck!'

'This is too much, sir…'

Meanwhile, Imran realized that his hands and feet had become sore from gripping the man. Actually, Imran was in sort of a daze. Imran untied his quarry's tie and tied his hands with it. Then he stood up and grabbed Hoopoe's neck. He said, 'You want to be unencumbered from this vocation?'

'Ye-yes ….' There was irritation in Hoopoe's tone but he did not try to free his neck from Imran's grip.

'Find the torch!' Imran yelled, pushing him to the ground and Hoopoe found the torch in an instant. It was lying at the spot where he had started at Imran's touch.

Imran trained the light on the man's face. He had fainted by now. He was a young and strong man, but his features were dissipated from a life of debauchery. He wore a black suit.

Chapter 10

ABOUT AN HOUR LATER Imran was interrogating the young man at the police station.

'Why had you gone there?'

'I don't know the reason.'

'You don't know or you won't tell?'

'Look sir, I am not hiding anything. By God, I don't know anything. The four of us were just told to stand outside. Only he was meant to go inside. Alone.'

'Who?'

'Safdar Khan.'

'Who is Safdar Khan?'

'You won't believe that we don't know anything about him, but he claims to be a landlord of some area and says that he is preparing a lawsuit against one of his rivals with our help... A few days ago we supposedly carried a body for a funeral from this very house. You'll be surprised to hear that beneath the shroud there were three buckets and one cauldron instead of a body. Yes...a fake funeral.'

'Wow!' Imran smiled.

'I will not hide anything, sir. He had given us four thousand rupees for these chores. Oh, and I forgot to tell you—he used to send us to an American's bungalow. That was also strange. Our job was just to create a hubbub there and come back. But he never told us why we had to do this.'

'What does Safdar Khan look like?'

'He has a thick beard, wears a shalwar and a long kameez, has a flat nose... Sleep dust in his eyes.'

'Does he wear dark glasses?' Imran asked.

'No. We have never seen him wearing glasses.'

'Okay, tell me the names and whereabouts of your other three accomplices.'

'I am not aware of anyone's name or whereabouts. When he gathers us at one place, that's the only time we see each other.

'Hmm. How does he contact you?'

'Over the phone. None of us know where he lives.'

'Do you know the phone numbers of the other three men?'

'No. We have never communicated with each other. We don't know each other, but we can easily recognize one another.'

Suddenly Imran stopped writing and closed the notebook. The culprit was sent to the lock-up.

Chapter 11

IT WAS A CLOUDY evening and darkness descended as soon as the sun set. By 11 pm it was impossible to see one's own hand. It was a still night; the kind that inspires a vague fear in people. But rain...there was no sign of rain.

Nawwab's Hashim's nephew Sajid was pacing about agitatedly, smoking one cigarette after another. A short while ago some policemen had visited him. One of them was an Intelligence Bureau officer. Sajid could not understand why the person claiming to be Nawwab Hashim had not been arrested yet. If he was indeed Nawwab Hashim then the police should have arrested him and questioned him about the corpse that was found in the haveli ten years ago.

But on the other hand the police also doubted Sajid. Nawwab Hashim had openly accused him of murder in Captain Fayyaz's office. Hashim had said that Sajid had murdered his friend Sajjad.

Sajid lit a new cigarette from the one he had almost finished and continued pacing up and down. There were two electric fans in the room, but he was still drenched in sweat. He wondered what would happen to him if the crime was proved to be committed by him. He had committed a grave mistake by letting that person reside in the bungalow. And now, for no apparent reason, the Intelligence Bureau insisted that he should be allowed to live in the haveli. Should he himself go somewhere else? But what would that achieve... This way the noose around his neck would be tightened even more.

Sajid sat down. He was tired. He didn't know what to do next. Sometimes he felt that he should actually commit murder—he should strangle that dubious man who was after his life and property. Throwing his cigarette, he lay down on the sofa with his shoes on and closed his eyes. But how was it possible to sleep in such a situation? He wanted to rest his tired mind. However, suddenly he heard a bizarre noise. He rushed to the lounge, baffled. But when he got there the place was deathly silent. However, his dogs were whimpering. Sajid couldn't understand what had caused that noise.

His heart was thumping. He stood in the porch for a while. He thought his ears were deceiving him. His tired mind was probably hallucinating. He had just turned to go back when the lawn echoed with the same noise. It seemed as if thousands of men had just screamed. The dogs started barking again. And now Sajid could also hear the sounds of fast approaching feet.

Two servants came running to him. They were panting heavily.

'Sir...what's going on?' one asked, gasping.

'How do I know! Go get torches from inside. Get all three rifles too. Hurry up! Gather all the servants. Go!'

Meanwhile, Nawwab Hashim, clad in sleeping attire, entered the lounge holding a rifle in his hand.

'Sajid!' he said. 'Are you pulling a new trick on me?'

'That's what I want to ask you, friend!' Sajid said, frowning and narrowing his eyes. 'Even if you are really my uncle, you cannot make me leave this haveli by playing tricks like these! I am not a coward. As long as I have ammunition in stock no one will be able to touch me, understand!'

'I understand everything,' Nawwab Hashim said. 'Even if you call ten thousand people I won't leave the haveli! Intelligence Bureau men watch over the haveli all the time. If there is even a scratch on my body, you will be in hell.'

'The thief blaming his captors. Great.' Sajid smiled bitterly.

In the meantime all the servants had gathered. There were eight in total. Three of them were men who had been hired to accompany Sajid on hunting expeditions—they were sharpshooters.

'I order you,' Sajid said to them, 'if you come across a stranger, shoot him without hesitation. I will take care of the rest.'

Carrying torches and rifles, the hunters rushed to the lawn.

'Take a few dogs with you as well. I can't accompany you right now. It is necessary for me to stay here.' And he glared at Nawwab Hashim.

'You cannot fool me like this!' Nawwab Hashim said.

'Oh, you can go to hell!' Sajid said, grinding his teeth. 'Why do I even need to fool you? If the police didn't want to keep you here, my servants would have grabbed you by your collar and kicked you out of the gate a long time ago!'

'Oh Sajid! Has your blood run thin!' Nawwab Hashim said, in pain and quite upset.

Suddenly they heard the noise again, but it didn't last for more than a moment. The dogs began barking again, and this was followed by the sound of running feet.

It was Sajid's servants rushing back pell-mell. They dashed back into the lounge, one or two fainting on the steps.

'Sir...no...one...no one at all! Only sounds...my God...sounds coming from the skies...from all four sides!'

'What is this nonsense?' Sajid shouted, agitated. 'Come, I'll go with you. Cowards! But if a bullet shatters my skull from behind then the person responsible for my death would be this man!' Sajid said, gesturing towards Nawwab Hashim. 'This person would be responsible for my death. All of you should remember him. Now come with me. Let me see what it is.'

Chapter 12

IMRAN WAS SLOUCHED IN his office chair. His eyes were half-closed and he was ruminatively chewing gum. Without bothering to open his eyes, he called Hoopoe.

'Ye-yes...You-Your Honour!' Hoopoe said, drawing near Imran.

'Sit down,' Imran said.

Hoopoe pulled a chair to Imran's table and sat down.

'Give me last night's report.'

'The-there...was quite a ru-ru-ruckus...all night... After regular intervals of time they made earth and heaven one with their cries...and this compounded with the howling of ebony tykes, my brain became an epicentre of utter dispersion and confusion.'

'Hoopoe, my dear man, speak to me in the language of men.'

'I al-al-always speak the nobleman's tongue.'

'I don't want to hear the nobleman's tongue. Talk to me in the language of human beings.'

'This matter...is be-beyond my...puh-perception and thought.'

'Okay. You get lost and send Shamshad.'

Hoopoe made a sour face. But he left silently, without voicing any objections. Shamshad entered after a while.

'Sit.' Imran pointed to the chair.

Shamshad sat down. From his appearance, he too seemed to be a fool.

'I need last night's report. Hurry up.'

'Last night!' Shamshad cried, drawing a deep breath. 'They made a lot of noise. They screamed so loudly that one couldn't even hear oneself. And sir, around 6 pm Nawwab Sajid's prostitute arrived. But her lady pimp was not with her. Her height must not be more than five feet. She was in an olive sari, and had Greek-style slippers on her feet. Eyes quite large...oval face...sharp features...'

'And your brain rotten!' Imran said, annoyed. 'Tell me if anyone came outside at night or not?'

'No, no one came out after the prostitute left.'

'Again that prostitute. Get out!' Imran roared, slamming his fist on the table.

Shamshad quietly got up and left.

Imran picked up the receiver of the phone.

'Hello, Super Fayyaz, Imran speaking.'

'Oh...Imran. Come over, my friend...a new joke! These wretches have truly made my life hell. I don't know what to do!'

'I will be there in a moment!' Imran said, standing up.

Fayyaz was alone in his room. But it was apparent that someone had just left.

'So? Didn't your men give you any peculiar news?' Fayyaz asked.

'One of them was just giving me some. Idiot. But I stopped him in the middle.'

'Sorry?'

'Nawwab Sajid's prostitute came. Height five feet tall. Features, olive sari, etcetera!'

'These wretches are also wasting their time with you!'

'Anyway, forget it,' Imran said seriously. 'What's your news?'

'Both of them were just here. They told me a new story. And both were accusing each other. Some mysterious sounds were heard in the haveli's compound through the night. They say that those sounds seemed to be coming from the sky. Sounds of thousands of men screaming simultaneously!'

'Yes, my men told me about it,' Imran said, nodding.

'Now both of them are accusing each other. What kind of sounds could those be?'

'I don't know, friend. We have heard such sounds before as well. You must remember that House of Fear case, don't you?'

'I remember it very well,' Fayyaz said, nodding. 'But that turned out to be a trick!'

'And you don't believe this to be a trick?' Imran asked.

'Sounds coming from the sky, son?'

'What do they both accuse each other of?'

'They think that one of them is responsible for the sounds.'

'And you don't want to accept it as a trick!'

'You don't understand me. I mean, which one of them could have pulled this trick?'

'Now you have jumped to another conclusion! My friend Fayyaz, this department is not at all suitable for you!'

'Shut up. Cut me some slack. You have become very conceited nowadays,' Fayyaz said bitterly. 'In this particular case, we will see what you are capable of.'

'Sure,' Imran said and left the room.

Chapter 13

Nawwab Sajid came out to the porch. In an attempt to allay his anxiety he had drunk a few pegs of whisky. Now his head was spinning. He fixed his gaze on the dark lawn.

'That was certainly an illusion,' he muttered.

But the next moment he heard a distinct whisper… Dilawar Ali…Dilawar Ali… It seemed as though the darkness outside had just found a voice. It was such a distinct whisper that it could easily have been heard a few furlongs away.

Sajid immediately sobered up.

The whispers were gradually getting louder. 'Dilawar Ali…Dilawar Ali.'

Then those whispers turned into a slightly husky voice. 'Dilawar Ali…Dilawar Ali…!' It seemed as if the person had been sobbing for a long time. The voice gradually became louder until it reached a crescendo. The voice saying Dilawar Ali broke into sobs and it did not seem like it was going to stop any time soon. Suddenly Sajid heard some gunshots, one after another, and then the crying ceased.

'I will hunt and kill each and every one of you,' Nawwab Hashim shouted at the darkness of the lawn. 'No one can scare me!'

Two more shots were fired.

'Dilawar Ali.' The whisper came again.

'You son of a...come out!' Nawwab Hashim roared.

A few more shots were fired.

In the meantime someone started banging at the gate. The gunshots stopped and the mysterious whisper was heard no more. Someone was banging at the gate with great energy.

'Open the gate... Police!' A voice came from outside. 'What's going on here?!'

Chapter 14

Nawwab Hashim and Nawwab Sajid were sitting in Captain Fayyaz's office. They both stared at each other murderously. It seemed as though they were going to kill each other at that very moment. Imran was pacing about the room. Captain Fayyaz, lost in thought, leaned back in his chair. It was apparent from Sajid's and Nawwab Hashim's faces that they had just been quarrelling.

'The question is, Nawwab Hashim Sahib,' Imran stopped pacing and said, 'why did you fire shots within city limits?'

'I was not in my senses!'

'Can I know the reason for this senselessness?'

'My God... What are you implying, Imran Sahib? If you were in my place what would you have done?'

'I would have hidden myself in a corner!' Imran replied seriously.

'I am not such a coward.'

'But you were fighting with thin air, Nawwab Sahib.'

'Wait a minute,' Sajid said suddenly, raising his hand. 'Have you accepted this impostor as Nawwab Hashim!'

'Tsk tsk...Sajid Sahab! Don't abuse your uncle,' Imran said.

'Conspiracy! By God, a conspiracy!' Nawwab Sajid murmured agitatedly.

'But today I have decided to put an end to this conspiracy!' Imran said, smiling. Nawwab Hashim and Sajid both gawked at him.

'Just tell us the story of your escape once more,' Imran said to Hashim.

'How many times do I have to repeat this story?' Nawwab Hashim cried wearily. 'Anyway... Where should I begin?'

'From the point your friend Sajjad enters this story.'

'Yes, Sajjad!' Nawwab Hashim said painfully, heaving a deep sigh.

'I'm waiting for you to begin,' Imran said when Hashim remained silent.

Nawwab Hashim wrinkled his forehead. It was as though he was trying to remember some long-forgotten story.

'Oh, ok... Sajjad arrived the same evening,' he murmured in a low voice. Then, addressing Imran, he began in a loud voice, 'The day that I planned to leave, Sajjad arrived... He didn't know anything. I did not tell him about my plan either. Then I silently left when he was still asleep.'

'But if the murder victim was indeed Sajjad, how come he was wearing your sleeping suit?' Imran asked.

'Oho! Imran Sahib! It's simple. The murderer, after realizing his mistake, made him Nawwab Hashim.'

'But after realizing his mistake why would he try to make Sajjad Nawwab Hashim? What was he to gain?'

'Nothing,' Nawwab Hashim said quickly. 'It is utterly useless to think about him. You should think about what he gains by declaring me dead,' he added, pointing to Sajjad.

'Oh! So you are trying to say that I am the murderer!' Sajid slammed his fist on the table.

'Wait, sir! You are not going to intervene!' Imran said, frowning at Sajid. Sajid murmured something and went silent.

'Yes, Nawwab Sahib,' Imran said to Nawwab Hashim. 'Tell me about Sajjad. What kind of a fellow was he and where did he live?'

'He was a vagabond, you know, the wandering poet type. He had no permanent place. Here today, gone tomorrow. He was very cultured and witty, though. That's why he was so warmly welcomed among the nobility.'

'Could you also tell me about his next of kin?'

'I can't say... He never mentioned any relatives.'

'But sir, could that body be declared your corpse merely on Sajid Sahib's identification?'

'The servants also identified it as his body,' Sajid interrupted, 'the servants who had lived with my late uncle for several years.'

'Where are those servants?' Nawwab Hashim roared. 'Have you retained even one of them?' He then said to Imran, 'When my own nephew had declared that it was my corpse, why would the servants speak against him and make themselves the target of the police investigations?' Then he turned to Sajid and said, 'And then if you indeed thought that the corpse was mine, why did you dismiss those servants! At least one or two of them should have been retained. Servants spend their whole lives in one household.'

'This point is indeed valid,' Imran said, nodding.

'So now not only do you want to appropriate my property but you also want to get me hanged!' Sajid said with a bitter smile.

'Are both these things impossible, Sajid Sahib?' Imran asked in all seriousness.

'Well, anything you have ever said is beyond my comprehension,' Sajid replied. 'Sometimes it seems that you are protecting me, and sometimes it seems that there is not much distance between me and the gallows!'

Before Imran could reply, Hashim interrupted. 'Listen Sajid, bribing can't work here. They are all dignified men. They are here to deliver justice.'

'You are wrong, Nawwab Sahib,' Imran said seriously. 'We are not here to deliver justice—justice is served by the court. Our task is only to recommend someone's neck for hanging. And let me decide now whose neck would be more appropriate for hanging in this case.'

Fayyaz was sitting quietly. All this time he hadn't tried to speak even once, but he knew that the decisive moment wasn't far.

Imran leaned forward and rang the bell on the table. Immediately, an attendant entered the room.

'Bring in the person... Got it?' Imran told the attendant.

'Yes sir,' the attendant said, and left.

The room had become deathly silent. It seemed as if it were a funeral gathering.

Both Nawwab Hashim and Nawwab Sajid looked crestfallen. Imran was staring at the floor as though the images on the carpet would somehow aid him in the matter at hand.

Suddenly they heard feet approaching, and the next moment Durdana was at the door. The attendant stood behind her, holding the door open.

Sajid's jaw dropped in astonishment and then closed. But Nawwab Hashim's disposition did not change. He merely glanced at her and then looked at Imran.

Durdana had stopped cold at the door. Her gaze was fixed on Nawwab Hashim's face and her eyes had widened. She looked apoplectic.

'Father!' A low scream escaped her mouth. And if Imran had not leaned forward to catch her, she would have fallen. She was in a swoon.

Imran sat her down in a chair.

'I don't understand what she means,' Nawwab Hashim said, frowning at Imran with bloodshot eyes.

'She did not call *me* father,' Imran said meaningfully.

'Wonderful! I see. Now I am being ensnared in a trap? Sajid, I'll sort you out!' Nawwab Hashim said threateningly.

'Quiet!' Fayyaz was annoyed. 'You can't threaten anyone in my office!'

'Yes! And I can be tricked into a trap before you? I did not expect this from you, sir... Anyway, I don't care. I will see who can trap me! The world knows that I did not marry anyone. Besides, no girl can reach the age of twenty in a mere ten years... Even if you bring not one, but a thousand girls who call me father you can't prove a thing... Huh!'

'But Captain Sahib,' Sajid addressed Fayyaz, 'can you see how closely they resemble each other?'

Fayyaz looked at the girl and then at Nawwab Hashim—indeed they did resemble each other very much. He was seeing Durdana for the first time.

'Oh Sajid... May you burn in hell!' Nawwab Hashim said, grinding his teeth.

'Oh, so has Sajid fathered this girl?' Sajid said smiling.

'Nawwab Hashim!' Imran said gravely. 'I affirm that you are Nawwab Hashim, and that Sajid cannot be the owner of your property in your lifetime.'

'Imran, you will drive me nuts!' Nawwab Hashim started laughing.

'Perhaps you are drunk,' Sajid said to Imran, irritated.

'No, Sajid Sahib! I am not drunk. It is true. You can be his heir only after Nawwab Hashim has been hanged.'

'Captain Sahib!' Nawwab Hashim shot up in anger. 'Is this your office or some bar filled with drunks?!'

'If *I* had said this you would've shot me.' Imran smiled at Fayyaz.

'What in the world are you up to, anyway?!' Fayyaz asked Imran angrily.

'Nawwab Sahib, take a seat. I was joking. I understand that you have suffered long, but what do we do about the fact that despite your attack on him, Hakim Moinuddin is still alive? It was I who got the news of his death published in the newspapers.'

'What nonsense!' Nawwab Hashim bellowed. 'I am going!'

'No, Your Honour,' Imran said, taking a revolver from his pocket and pointing it at Nawwab Hashim. 'You will not go but you will be escorted. Take a seat. Could you tell us why you were firing frantically upon hearing Dilawar Ali's name last night?'

'Get out of my way!' Nawwab Hashim said in anger. He leaped towards the door. Imran's leg shot out instantly to block his path. Nawwab Hashim fell on his face and Imran put his right foot on his back.

Durdana, who had come to her senses by now, screamed and ran to Imran. 'What are you doing! My heart tells me that Father is alive!'

'He is not your father!' said Imran, who was exerting all his strength to hold Nawwab Hashim down.

'He is my father. He has just shaved off his beard. For God's sake, let go of him.'

'No, my dear. I will explain everything to you.'

Nawwab Hashim clasped Imran's leg. Instantly, Imran's knee was on his neck and Nawab Hashim was groaning in pain.

'Fayyaz! Handcuffs!' Imran cried.

Fayyaz got up from his desk, albeit hesitantly. He called the attendant. Meanwhile, Nawwab Hashim freed himself from Imran's grip. Imran toppled over, but he did not let go of Nawwab Hashim's leg.

In the meantime, the attendants overpowered Nawwab Hashim and handcuffed him.

'You will all pay for this!' Nawwab Hashim cried as he stood up, panting.

'Sit down!' Imran pushed him into a chair. Then he turned to the girl, who was standing nearby and trembling fearfully.

'What was your father's name?' Imran asked the girl.

'Dilawar Ali,' the girl said in a choked voice.

'But this is Nawwab Hashim!'

Durdana did not say anything. Imran signalled her to sit down. She sat down, trembling.

'Nawwab Hashim,' Imran said 'I charge you with fraud, murder, and attempted murder.'

'Do as you please. I will deal with these charges in court,' Nawwab Hashim said impudently.

'You are the murderer of this girl's father, Dilawar Ali, who resembled you a great deal. You murdered him ten years ago. People mistakenly identified his body as yours and this happened because of the resemblance. You disappeared for four years, came back and housed yourself in Dilawar Ali's home. The girl was also deceived because of the resemblance.'

'A fable from *A Thousand and One Nights*!' Nawwab Hashim laughed madly.

'Okay, then listen to the complete fable! Dilawar Ali was the illegitimate child of your father, and had the same countenance as yours. His mother died when he was a child. Your father loved her a lot. To save the child from your mother's ill treatment, he removed him from the city. He was raised in a boarding school in Dilawarpur. He was a very virtuous man, and a connoisseur of knowledge and art. When he reached adulthood he realized his position and decided to avoid this city. Your father supported him throughout. He also gave him some family antiques. And that jewellery box, which you duplicated and for which you appropriated twenty-five thousand from Moody, was one of them... Am I saying anything wrong? Nawwab Hashim, you cannot pronounce any of this wrong. I have gathered tons of evidence against you!'

'Keep blabbering,' Nawwab Hashim said, making a sour face. 'Who will believe this nonsense?'

'Okay, so Fayyaz Sahib,' Imran addressed Fayyaz, 'now I am coming to the part of the story where Nawwab Hashim and Dilawar accidentally crossed each other's path. This came to pass because of a woman, who was Nawwab Hashim's lover—and it is true that she had first met Nawwab Hashim. Then somehow that woman reached Dilawarpur, where she met Dilawar Ali whose countenance was exactly like Nawwab Hashim's. At first she took him for Nawwab Hashim and treated him very candidly. But her misunderstanding was rectified a long while later when Nawwab Hashim and Dilawar Ali came face to face. Both the men were of the same age. Nawwab

Hashim knew about Dilawar Ali but they had met for the first time—and this very meeting became the reason for their animosity towards each other. That woman had taken a great liking to Dilawar Ali—his habits and manners were those of a nobleman's and his intellectual capabilities far outpaced Nawwab Hashim's. The woman decided to marry Dilawar Ali!

'Nawwab Hashim was cut to the quick but he remained silent. However, the flame of vengeance kept burning in his heart. The woman died a year later. But in the interim she had given birth to a daughter.' Imran pointed to Durdana and paused. Nawwab Hashim was smiling as if some ignorant child was blabbering before him.

'Ten years ago, when Durdana was ten years old, Nawwab Hashim hatched a plan. He wanted to avenge his defeat in any case. First, he made one of his mistresses run away with a coachman. Then he murdered Dilawar Ali, put his body in his bed, and fled. It was the time of war. He got a job in the army and was sent across the ocean. He returned four years later and because he had the same countenance as Dilawar Ali's he did not face any problem in playing his role. But till when could he continue doing this? He had to say goodbye to his penurious life one day and return to his haveli. But coming back to the haveli was not easy. Sajid now possessed the property. He would have needed to move heaven and earth to annul Sajid's ownership. He would have needed a lot of money. That was why Nawwab Hashim duplicated the jewellery box and sent Durdana to Dilawarpur. When she came back Nawwab Hashim had changed his identity. He informed the girl of her father's death and presented himself as her father's friend. The girl was deceived. Then he used her to trap Moody, who bought the fake jewellery box for twenty-five thousand. The girl brought the money back home and Nawwab Hashim stole it. The original jewellery box and the money are still in his possession.'

'One minute,' Fayyaz interrupted, raising his hand. 'How did you learn all these things?'

'From Hakim Moinuddin, a resident of Dilawarpur, who was one of the closest friends of this girl's father. He knew Dilawar Ali intimately and was well aware of his life's circumstances. When Durdana told me about him, I went to see him. But I found him lying unconscious, wounded by a dagger. Someone had attacked him and had left him there, thinking him dead. But in actuality the wound was not serious. He survived. But I still got the news of his murder published in Dilawarpur's newspapers. I learnt of this situation from him.'

'I don't know any Hakim Moinuddin,' Nawwab Hashim said. 'All of this is nonsense and Sajid's conspiracy. Money has a lot of power. Not all the people in the world can be fooled. Even identical twins don't resemble each other to the extent that a daughter takes a man who is not her father to be her father... Sajid, these base tactics won't help you in court!'

'We can retrieve Dilawar Ali's photos from Dilawarpur's boarding school, where he was raised,' Imran said.

'Those will be my photographs,' Nawwab Hashim said, 'which Sajid must have found easily. And now, he is using them in this conspiracy.'

'Wait, Imran,' Fayyaz interrupted. 'If the purpose was to murder Dilawar Ali, why was it done in such a complicated way? What was the benefit of doing it this way? Why couldn't it have been done in any other way?'

'Caught you, haven't we?' Nawwab Hashim said mockingly and began laughing.

'After his murder,' Imran said, 'his photos would have been in the newspaper. The police would have certainly been startled at his resemblance to one of the city's aristocrats, and what would have then followed is apparent.'

'Again this discussion of resemblances!' Nawwab Hashim said, making a sour face. 'Who will believe this story? The scheme is indeed very clever but it will not succeed. And I want to set the record straight. The photo that Imran produces of this fictitious Dilawar Ali will be of me. Just now this girl mentioned a beard, therefore, I want to make it clear that once I too had grown a beard and I also had several photographs of it.'

'So you are hell bent on proving me wrong, Nawwab Hashim,' Imran said smiling. 'May I tell you… That day you burnt a collection of documents in Dilawar Ali's house. But the thing which you hoped to burn in this fire was not part of the lot. You were not sure if it was burnt or not. That's why you have been trying to enter that yellow house with your four men—to look for that thing. But you couldn't find it! It is in my possession now!'

'What?' Nawwab Hashim said anxiously. Then suddenly he got hold of himself and laughed mockingly at Imran.

'For your information I will only state that Dilawar Ali was a keen daguerreotype maker,' Imran said. Nawwab Hashim's face darkened immediately. He licked his dry lips.

'Captain Fayyaz,' Imran said with a smile, 'about fifteen years ago, Dilawar Ali had prepared a daguerreotype of an announcement by the Viceroy, which was published by a government monthly committed to war propaganda. And along with that print, photos of those working for that monthly were also published. You can find a photograph of Dilawar the daguerreotype maker in that monthly. Nawwab Hashim was in search of that monthly. But I found it instead.'

Nawwab Hashim looked defeated... He looked at Imran fearfully. He was completely dumbfounded.

'So Nawwab Hashim,' Imran said with a playful smile, 'last night, why did you fire blindly upon hearing Dilawar Ali's name?'

'What the devil was that?' Sajid asked.

'That devil was Imran,' Imran said seriously. 'I had fixed tiny speakers on the trees in your lawn and I was broadcasting a ghost show for his benefit.'

Chapter 15

ABOUT A MONTH LATER Nawwab Sajid and Durdana were strolling in the lawn of the haveli.

'I am telling you again, you have made a mistake in marrying me,' Durdana said.

'No, dear! I have done a wise thing for the first time in my life,' Sajid replied with a smile.

'You will think one day...you will have to...that "I wish my wife was of noble birth."'

'For me, it is enough that you are the daughter of a virtuous and honest man. You have seen the deeds of my "noble" uncle. He wanted to get me hanged for a sin I hadn't committed. Just to save his neck! Your father was certainly a better human being than him.'

'All that is fine, but I don't know why my heart still grieves for Nawwab Sahib.'

'Oho!' Nawwab Sajid laughed loudly. 'You also seem to be more than virtuous, like your father. But Uncle cannot be saved from the scaffold! Imran has trapped him from all four sides... Oh, what a tremendous fellow this Imran is! He traps you in the blink of an eye, and until the end you don't know whether you are being exonerated or indicted... Aha!

We completely forgot about poor Moody... I am thinking something, dear... I need your advice.'

'Tell me, what is it?'

'We have already returned Moody his money. Why don't we also present him the original jewellery box as a gift? He is so nice; if he were even a little churlish, you would have been rotting in jail right now.'

'I too was thinking the same,' Durdana said with a smile.

'Okay then, let's invite him home tomorrow.'

'Invite Imran Sahib as well.'

'No... He refuses to even recognize me now. I was very embarrassed at the club yesterday. I greeted him with great enthusiasm. But he was very cold. He said, "Excuse me, do I know you?"'

Durdana burst out laughing.

A DANGEROUS MAN

Chapter 1

ROSHI HAD BEEN STARING at him for quite some time. He had entered the restaurant at the ABC Hotel early in the evening and it was now seven. The wind blowing from the sea had subsided.

All the tables except the one on which Roshi was sitting were empty when he had entered. But now there was no space for even an ant.

He was a handsome, well-dressed young man. But this wasn't something that would draw Roshi's attention towards him. She had spent hundreds of nights with dozens of beautiful men in this very hotel. And she had long lost that inexplicable feeling which attracts a woman to a man.

Roshi was an Anglo-Burmese woman. She must have been a girl at some point—but that was a long time ago. It was around the time when the Japanese bombed Singapore, and everyone had run helter-skelter. Roshi was a fourteen-year-old girl at that time. Her father was an established trader in Singapore. But being the daughter of an accomplished trader did not mean that after starving for three days, the girl in Roshi would not be forced to turn into a woman for a mere cup of tea! It is quite possible that her father did not get even a cup of tea, for of course he did not have the ability to turn into a girl, let alone into a woman... Anyway, Roshi had no idea what became of him. And now she was a mature woman of twenty-five... She was not the same Roshi of eleven years ago...but she still remembered that cup of tea... And since then she had made numerous men go bankrupt, so much so that they were reduced to begging for a cup of tea.

Now she had a sumptuous, high-class flat. She had all the comforts of the world, and she knew that she would never have to beg for another meal.

This hotel was feasible for her business and most of her nights were spent here. It was near a port and foreigners—most of whom were white Caucasians—frequented it day and night. And it was thanks to them that this hotel ran successfully because the natives never came this way. But Roshi was not interested in the young man because he was an unusual guest at the hotel, which was usually frequented by sailors.

He had been acting foolishly since he had arrived. As soon as the waiter saluted the young man—all the waiters considered it necessary to greet every guest, whether new or old, in the same manner—not only did he reciprocate the greeting but also shook hands with the waiter reverently and enquired in detail for quite some time about the waiter's and his family's well-being.

First he ordered tea but then sat quietly until the tea was cold. He took a sip, and made a sour face upon tasting it. He then returned the tea and ordered coffee instead. Perhaps he found the coffee more distasteful than cold tea, for he made a face as though suppressing the urge to vomit. Then he returned the coffee as well, and hurriedly downed several glasses of water.

It was now dark outside and the lights were switched on in the hotel. But perhaps that stupid young man had sworn not to leave.

Roshi's interest increased. She stayed firmly in her place, discarding any plans of leaving.

The table covers were changed before dinner time and glasses with napkins tucked in them were placed on the tables along with vases of moist, fresh flowers.

That stupid young man had pulled his chair back and one of the waiters was setting his table. As soon as the waiter left, he took a rose from the vase and began to sniff it. He seemed to be lost in thought and he had not once bothered to look around him. Perhaps he felt lonely.

Roshi continued gazing at him and now, God alone knew why, she was beginning to feel peculiarly attracted towards him. She thought of leaving several times but could not bring herself to do so.

Meanwhile, it was time for dinner and the young man ordered food. He absently caressed the flower. He smelt it occasionally, and sometimes, closing his eyes, he stroked his cheeks with it as if practising a sacred ritual. The food was served, but he remained motionless. Lost in thought, he seemed completely unaware of the waiter's presence and of the food.

Roshi couldn't stop looking at him. Suddenly he dipped the rose in the gravy—and began to chew it! He then made such a sour face that Roshi burst out laughing spontaneously. Crushed flower petals were slipping out of the young man's mouth.

'Boy!' he cried in a whiny voice to summon the waiter and many people looked at him, startled. The dining hall was very crowded now. Perhaps only about five tables were free.

'Everything is ruined,' he said gloomily. 'Take it away...bring the bill.'

'What's the matter, sir?' the waiter asked respectfully.

'Nothing...it is my fate... I am unable to enjoy anything today,' the young man said piteously. 'Bring me the bill.'

The waiter collected the dishes and went off. He soon returned. The young man glanced at the slip on the tray and began to search his pockets. Then, lo and behold, he pulled out several wads of notes from his pockets, put them on the table, and stood up. He then began to search his inner pockets.

Finally he took out a loosened wad, drew out a hundred-rupee note from it, and put the note on the tray.

Roshi's eyes widened in wonder. The young man was carelessly stuffing the bundles of money into the pockets of his coat.

Roshi looked around and saw that all the people in the dining hall were staring at the young man. She also spotted some rogues gazing at him greedily.

Roshi got up from her place and slowly walked towards the table of that foolish man. She knew what was going to happen to him. The room next to the dining hall was a grand casino—she knew that in no time some agents would charm him to that room... and in a few hours he would lose every penny.

'Hey Parrot, how are you?' said Roshi, putting her hand affectionately on the young man's shoulder, as though they were the best of friends.

The young man, startled, looked at her stupidly. His lips were parted and his eyes widened in surprise.

'Now, don't tell me that you don't recognize me,' Roshi said coquettishly, pulling a chair and sitting down. Seated at a distance, the casino agents exchanged smiles.

'Aha, can't you speak?' Roshi addressed him again.

'I...dou....happ,' the young man stammered.

'I think you are crazy,' she said, putting her elbows on the table and leaning forward. 'Flaunting your wealth in this dangerous place cannot mean anything else.'

'Dangerous place!' The young man widened his eyes and leaned back in his chair.

'Yes, my Parrot. Is it your first time here?'

The young man nodded.

'Why have you come here?'

'Someone had promised to meet me here,' the young man said shyly.

'Who is it—some girl?'

The young man nodded again. But, bashful, this time he could not look directly into Roshi's eyes. He was blushing like an unmarried Indian girl who had overheard someone discussing her marriage.

Roshi looked at him compassionately.

'If she promised to meet you here, she can't be a good girl!'

'Why?' said the young man, surprised.

'But tell me, why are you carrying around so much money?' Roshi said, ignoring his question.

'I usually don't leave home until I have this much cash with me.'

Suddenly an agent signalled Roshi secretively. He was asking her to take him to the casino. But Roshi turned her face away.

'Then it is quite possible that this might be the last night of your life,' Roshi said to the young man.

'Why are you scaring me for no reason!' the young man said fearfully. 'I'm already an unfortunate man. I can't even eat properly. Some things are cold and some things bitter—this is such a third-class restaurant. Even the wayside inn in my grandfather's village serves much better food.'

Roshi looked at him in amazement. He remained silent for a while, then stood up and said, 'Okay, I shall leave now.'

'Perhaps you are not from this city!' Roshi said. She sounded apprehensive.

'Do you also have knowledge of hidden things!' The young man was astonished. He sat down again.

'You will have to cross a desolate area to reach the road from here,' Roshi said. 'It is quite possible that you don't even get a chance to scream before a few inches of cold metal slice into your body.'

'I don't understand.'

'You'll be killed, idiot!' Roshi said, grinding her teeth. 'Haven't you heard about the terrible crimes being perpetrated in this area?'

'I don't know anything,' the young man said, shifting restlessly.

'What time was the girl supposed to be here?'

'Oh, it's eight now! She had promised to see me at seven!'

'How long have you known her?'

'Since yesterday.'

'What!'

'Yes, yes, since yesterday. I met her yesterday at the railway station waiting room.'

'And you came running here today? You're really an idiot.'

'The thing is...that...th...'

'Don't talk nonsense. Either way, you are in grave danger. But your life is safe in one case—that is if you stay here. However, you will definitely be robbed in both.'

'I don't understand anything that you are saying.'

'A dangerous man reigns over the darkness spread outside, and he often murders someone or the other just for fun! But you...you are a golden bird, so you'll have to wash your hands off both your money and your life.'

'Oh, I am in deep trouble...' the young man said sorrowfully.

'Keep sitting here until I ask you to do otherwise,' Roshi said.

'But you mentioned some danger here as well.'

'You will be robbed here, dear Parrot,' Roshi said with a smile, blinking her eyes. 'That, over there, is a casino. And the casino agents are on the lookout for you.'

'Good...good...' the dimwit said, laughing, 'that is wonderful news! I would like to gamble! Take me there!'

'Oh! I get it now. So you are here to gamble!'

'No...that's not true... God! She is not here yet... And I can swear I didn't come here with any intention to gamble! But now I will definitely do so. One doesn't get such opportunities very often!'

'So you aren't really a gambler?'

'No! I don't even know how to gamble.'

'Then how will you play?'

'Somehow! I just want to play once for the experience. I'm telling you the truth, I won't get such an opportunity again.'

'What kind of an opportunity?'

'The thing is,' the dimwit, leaning forward, said secretively, 'Daddy and Mummy are not here!'

Roshi burst into spontaneous laughter. But when she saw that this foolish man was serious she became serious as well. And strangely enough, at that moment, she began to feel like a fool herself.

'Daddy and Mummy,' the young man spoke again, 'have imposed strong restrictions on me. But I want to see the world. I am a grown-up man now, you know... See, she hasn't arrived yet...'

'I won't let you gamble, do you understand!'

'Why?! Wonderful...that's great! Who are you to stop me? I haven't even seen you before today!'

'You won't gamble!' Roshi said, biting her upper lip.

'Let's see how you stop me!'

In the meantime, an agent of the casino got up from his table and came towards them. He looked dangerous. He had a thick beard and a moustache, and his teeth were visible through his slightly parted lips. His eyes were ferocious. Pulling up a chair, he sat facing Roshi.

'Is he your friend?' he asked her.

'Yes!' Roshi replied harshly.

'Has he come here for the first time?'

'Yes...yes!' Roshi said, annoyed.

'You sound upset,' he observed in an affectionate tone.

'Go! Mind your own business! He is not a gambler!'

'I am definitely going to play!' The idiot slammed his fist on the table. 'You can't stop me! Got it?!'

'Oh, I see.' The agent stared at Roshi. His eyes were vengeful. Then he turned to the idiot and said, 'No, mister, no one can stop you. Fortunate young men like you pocket thousands of rupees from here every day. And this broad forehead of yours...aha-ha! It's a sign of success and good fortune! Come with me. I will tell you the secrets of winning. I'll just take 15 per cent commission—if you win, that is! So that is fine, no?'

'That's perfectly fine, my friend!' said the idiot, slapping the open palm of the agent. 'Let's go.'

Roshi was left sitting there, as both of them got up and left for the casino.

Chapter 2

Roshi was weary for no reason. She felt hurt. Only God knew why. She kept sitting where she was. A storm raged within her. It was very strange. It was her first meeting with him. And that, too, a forced one! Despite this she felt as if that dimwit's behaviour had ruined a long friendship. Why didn't he listen to her? Why did he disregard her advice?

She began to laugh at her stupidity. After all, who was she to stop him? She didn't know who he was, where he had come from, where he would be the next day. If feeling this way about such a person wasn't stupidity, then what was? She had met, not one, but hundreds of men before him, and she had had no pity in her heart for them even when she heartlessly took advantage of them. But God only knows why her humanity had been kindled on seeing that hapless young man being ripped off! She felt as though a fatuous son of hers had broken her heart.

'Let him go to hell!' she murmured softly, called the waiter, and ordered a whisky. Then she shook her head as though trying to get rid of that dimwit's image from it. She thought she would get up as soon as her drink was over. But despite her firm resolve she continued sitting there...thinking about the stupid young man. An hour passed. And then she saw him again.

Standing at the casino's door he was wiping sweat from his face. Their eyes met, and he shot to her table like an arrow.

'You were right!' he said, panting, as he sat on a chair. 'I lost three thousand rupees!'

Roshi frowned at him for a while, then, grinding her teeth, she said, 'Go...go away...or I'll give you a tight slap!'

'No, I won't go...you said that it is dangerous outside!'

Roshi was silent. She was pondering something.

'Tell me, what should I do?' The idiot spoke again.

'Go to hell.'

'I am such an ass.' The idiot looked at Roshi and said to himself, 'I mean, how will *this* poor soul sitting before me tell me anything?'

The idiot stood up and left the table.

Roshi was extremely annoyed. She didn't care about him in the least. But she couldn't help keeping her eyes on him until he walked out of sight.

Suddenly a thought crossed her mind and she was concerned for him again. It occurred to her that it was a dark moonless night and that idiot was wandering out alone! He had lost three thousand but even so he must have a lot of cash in his pocket. He had several wads of high denomination notes. He must have thirty to forty thousand on him...perhaps even more!

She quickly picked up her handbag and left the hotel. Darkness reigned outside. She could see a dark shadow at some distance. A moving shadow...who could be none other than that idiot. There were small hillocks ahead, and dense bushes spread for miles on the left. In order to reach the main road crossing those mounds was unavoidable. But considering the current safety situation and the time of the day, this was not advisable. Even the police had declared it a dangerous zone!

Roshi was chastising herself. Why didn't she stop him from going there? Why didn't she tell him the way to the port? Now she was in another dilemma. She didn't know how to call him—she didn't even know his name.

Suddenly she saw another shadow emerge quickly from behind a mound and begin to follow the first one. Then she saw it pouncing on the first shadow—and a scream slipped out of her lips, travelling far in the dark. It was a while before she got hold of herself.

Entangled, both shadows fell to the ground. A gunshot was heard and one of the shadows jumped up and ran into the surrounding thicket.

Roshi ran towards the scene anxiously.

She saw a man lying on the ground under the stars; the second man had disappeared. She was sure that he could not be anyone other than that stupid man. 'What happened?' She bent over him nervously.

'I feel sleepy,' the idiot replied in a quavering voice.

'Get up!' She began to shake him forcefully. 'Run! Run to the hotel with all your might!'

The idiot jumped up, very briskly lifted Roshi to his shoulder, and started running towards the hotel. Roshi was left exclaiming, 'Oh...oh...!'

Shortly, the two of them were standing before each other and gasping. They were near the central gate of the hotel. A crowd had already gathered there because of the gunfire and Roshi's scream.

'Are you hurt anywhere?' Roshi asked.

'I am not hurt anywhere, but I've received a big blow—I have lost every penny I had!'

The manager of the hotel brought them inside and took them straight to his room.

'You have committed a huge mistake!' he said to the idiot.

'Oh sir, I took the same route in the evening!'

'Did you not see the signboard at the corner of the street which says that the life and property of those venturing to that place after 7 pm cannot be protected? This board has been put up by the police department!'

'I didn't see it.'

'How much did you lose?' the manager asked sympathetically.

'Forty-seven thousand!'

'My God!' The manager's eyes widened in astonishment.

'And three thousand in your casino...' he continued.

'I'm sorry,' the manager said regretfully, 'but gambling is really a matter of fate. You lost three thousand today but you may win six tomorrow.'

'Get up,' Roshi said, pulling the idiot's hand.

They walked out of the manager's room. People started gathering around them once again, but Roshi lost no time in shrugging them off.

Exiting from the hotel's back door, they walked towards the port.

'So Parrot, what is the plan now?' Roshi asked him.

'The plan is that I won't leave this place before recovering my money! Fifty thousand rupees is not a small amount...'

'But why did you bring so much money at all?'

'I had to buy fifty buffaloes.'

'Buffaloes?!'

'Yes, buffaloes. I can't go back without them because my daddy is very hotheaded!'

'Is he a buffalo trader?'

'No. He is in love with them!' the idiot said seriously, and Roshi burst into laughter.

'Huh? Do you think I'm joking?' the idiot said, surprised. 'It is true that he is elated when he sees a lot of buffaloes around him!'

'What else does he do? I mean, what does he do for a living?'

'Erm...that I don't know.'

'Are you crazy or something?' Roshi asked.

'I don't know.'

'How much money do you have now?'

'About a quarter maybe! Don't worry about the money. I will recover each and every penny!'

'From whom?'

'The one who has snatched it. Who else?!'

'Parrot, you are a complete ass!' Roshi began laughing. 'I don't know how you are still alive. That person never leaves his quarry alive.'

'Who is he after all?'

'No one knows. Policemen tremble at the idea of stepping into that area! God knows how many police officers he has killed so far.'

'Maybe...but I will recover my money, I know.'

'But how, you old Parrot?'

'I'll hide in those bushes early in the evening tomorrow.'

Roshi burst into laughter. 'Parrot, you are actually crazy!' she said. 'Tell me, where are you staying?'

'Hotel Lebraska.'

'But you are broke now. How will you stay there?'

'That's not a problem. I can stay the night at a shelter, but to return without the buffaloes is out of the question!'

Roshi was silent. As they neared the port she signalled a taxi to stop.

'Come, sit.'

'I am hungry!'

'So now you want me to pay for your food?!' Roshi said, shoving him into the taxi.

The two of them got in and the cab started moving.

'Don't presume that I am penniless. I said that I have a quarter in my pocket! But wait, I am not a fool—when travelling, I don't keep all my money in one place.'

The idiot began to untie his shoelaces. He took both his shoes off, held them upside down, and began to shake them. The next moment he had two wads of notes in his hand.

'These are two and a half thousand,' the idiot said ingenuously.

'And what if I snatch them now?' Roshi said with a smile.

'You cannot do that. I will scare you away.'

'Scare me?'

'Yes. I have a revolver. And I also fired at the thief.'

'Do you have a licence for it?'

'I don't care about licences and other such formalities... See, I'm not lying.' The idiot took out a revolver from his pocket and held it out to Roshi. She guffawed.

The 'revolver' had a coil of crackers wrapped round its barrel—it was just a cheap toy gun.

'Parrot,' she said seriously, 'I don't understand what species of men you belong to.'

'Listen! This is too much!' the idiot said angrily. 'You've been calling me Parrot all this time and I haven't said a word...and now you are calling me an animal!'

'No! When did I call you an animal?'

'Then what does species mean? Buffaloes are my father's weakness, not mine!'

'But still, you look a lot like a parrot,' Roshi said teasingly.

'Of course not! You are a liar. You can't prove that I look like a parrot.'

'I will do that some other time. Tell me that you...' Her voice turned into a scream before she could complete the sentence. A bullet had been fired from a passing car.

'Stop...driver...stop!' the idiot yelled.

The car stopped with a jolt. The driver was terrified.

The other car disappeared, whizzing into the darkness. Its taillights were missing, so one could see nothing.

The idiot bent over Roshi. 'Woman...O woman...er...gi...girl!' he said as he shook her fiercely.

Roshi's eyes were open. She was trembling like a baby bird who had fallen from its nest. She couldn't say a word.

'Say something...did the bullet hit you?'

Roshi shook her head.

She was terrified. She had seen the flash of the gunshot in the window of the passing car... And then heard the bang of the gunshot... The bullet had perhaps slid off the taxi's roof.

'What was that, sir?' the driver asked, frightened.

'A cracker!' the idiot said, shaking his head. 'One of my naughty friends has played a prank. Now come on, start moving! Yes...but switch off the interior light. Otherwise he will play the same prank again!'

Then, patting Roshi's shoulder, he said, 'Tell me your address so I can take you home.'

Roshi collected herself and sat up carefully. She was still breathing heavily.

'Can he be the same person?' the idiot asked her softly.

'I don't know,' Roshi said, panting.

'I guess he's after me for good now...?' the idiot asked ingenuously.

'Oh...Parrot! Now my life is in danger too!'

'Huh? Why yours?'

'He is crazy. Whoever he is after, he kills them without fail. There have been cases in which people who survived the first attack were killed in a second one.'

'Who is he after all? And what does he want? He has already snatched my money. What does he want now?'

'I don't know who he is and what he wants. But anyway, all this has happened only because of your stupidity.'

'So did you want me to die without putting up a fight?' the idiot asked artlessly.

'No, Parrot! But you shouldn't have shown off your wealth like that.'

'I didn't know they would even eye such a meagre amount as fifty thousand rupees.'

'You think it's meagre?!' Roshi said, astonished. 'Never in my life have I seen this much money together... Parrot, are you a man or a money-making machine...'

'Forget that. You were saying that you are in danger?'

'Yes, that's true.'

'If you permit me, perhaps I can spend the night with you?'

'Oh Parrot...of course...of course... I've also noticed one thing: despite being a complete parrot you are absolutely carefree and brave! But I still can't understand your revolver—what use is it?!'

'Okay, so then—I'm coming with you! But will I get anything to eat at your place?'

Chapter 3

'See, here is my tiny flat,' Roshi said.

They entered the flat, and the idiot flopped onto a sofa as though he had always lived there.

'This place would be wonderful if I could also get something to eat!' the idiot said in all seriousness.

'You'll have to help me with that! I live here alone.'

About an hour later they were at the dining table and the idiot was stuffing himself as if it were his last meal.

'I am enjoying it now,' he said, chewing. 'The food at that hotel is atrocious.'

'Parrot...are you really what you seem to be?' She looked at him intently.

'I don't understand.'

'Nothing... Oh! I haven't asked you your name yet!'

'You can ask me now...but I don't like my name at all.'

'What is it?'

'Imran...Ali Imran.'

'What do you do?'

'I spend. And when I don't have money, I keep my shirt on.'

'Where does the money come from?'

'Ah...' Imran heaved a sigh. 'This is a very difficult question. If someone asked me this in an interview I will have to bid goodbye to the job. Since my childhood I have always wondered where money comes from! But alas! I haven't been able to find an answer! When I was little, I used to think that perhaps pressed coins are found in biscuits.'

'Okay, so you don't want to tell me anything about yourself.'

'I have told you everything about myself. But you are mostly asking things which are concerned not with me but with my daddy!'

'I see! It means that you don't do anything yourself.'

'Urgh...! Right...absolutely right! Sometimes my mind strays and I become inattentive... Perhaps I should have given the same answer to your question! Okay, what is your name?'

'Roshi.'

'That's right! You even look Roshi going by your face!'

'What do you mean?'

'Again that difficult question! I cannot explain everything that slips off my tongue. Just like that. I don't know what it is... Perhaps I should have said that like you, your name is also...what is it... Oho! What do you call it! What nonsense! That word was on the tip of my tongue just now...it has disappeared now!'

Imran began rubbing his forehead helplessly.

Roshi was looking at him strangely. She did not know what to make of him—whether he was half-crazy or someone very cunning. But she did not have reasonable evidence to think of him as clever. If he was clever, how did he lose so much money?

'Things are gradually becoming clear to me now.' Imran heaved a sigh. 'The girl whom I met in the waiting room must be that scoundrel's agent! Yes... What else? Otherwise, why would she call me to the hotel? But Joshi...er...what's your name... Oh... Roshi...Roshi! I liked that girl...but I like *you* now! I deeply regret that I didn't listen to you... Won't you help me now?'

Roshi was smiling charmingly.

'How can I help?' she asked.

'Look Roshi...*Roshi*...this is certainly a wonderful name. It seems to slide off my tongue like honey... Roshi... Wow... Ah! So, yes, Roshi, I want to retrieve my lost money.'

'It's impossible! You are talking like a child. You haven't deposited that money in a bank that you can get it back!'

'Nothing's impossible if a man tries! Aha...aha... haven't you read Napoleon's biography?'

'My Parrot!' Roshi said, laughing. 'Why did you step out of the cradle so soon?!'

'I am not in a mood to joke!' Imran said, like a petulant child.

Roshi guffawed. She was acting exactly as though she was teasing a doltish child.

'Okay, I am leaving,' Imran said, irritated.

'Wait! Wait!' She was serious immediately. 'Okay, tell me, what were you saying?'

'No, I won't!' Imran said, sitting down. 'I'll deal with it without anyone's advice!'

'No, tell me, what do you want to do?'

'How many times do I have to bellow that I want to recover my money from him?!'

'It's fanciful thinking! Puerility!' Roshi said thoughtfully. 'Even the police haven't had any luck in that area—they gave up in the end and put up that danger sign there instead.'

'Doesn't the hotel management know anything about him either?' Imran asked.

'I can't say anything with certainty.'

'The police must have investigated them.'

'Of course! A group of policemen had been posted at the hotel for quite a while. But despite that the dangerous man was able to carry out his deeds without a problem.'

'Roshi, Roshi! You cannot prevent me from nabbing him!' Imran began to get animated. 'I won't leave this place until I've sorted him out.'

'What nonsense!' Roshi was getting irritated. She said, 'Go and sleep in that room. There is only one bed. I will sleep here, on the sofa.'

'No. You go to your bed. I'll sleep on the sofa,' Imran replied.

They started arguing about this. Eventually, Imran had to go to the bedroom and Roshi lay down on the sofa.

It was a mildly cold night. So she pulled a light blanket over herself. She was still thinking about Imran. But the fear of that dangerous unknown man also haunted her.

Who was that man? Even the police of Shadabnagar did not have the answer to this question. He had committed numerous offences so far, but the police had been unsuccessful in capturing him. And strangest of all was the fact that he carried out his crimes only in one particular area—he never targeted any other area of the city.

Roshi continued thinking about him and tried hard not to fall asleep. She was afraid that he might come there. That was why she hadn't turned off the lights. Whenever she was about to fall asleep she'd think she'd heard a gunshot, and her eyes would open with a start.

The clock struck two. Suddenly she sat up nervously. God only knows why she felt she was in danger. She kept staring around fearfully for a few moments. Then she got up from the sofa, and tiptoed to the door of the room in which the idiot was sleeping.

She put her hand on the door and pushed it slightly. The door opened. Her eyes widened in astonishment—the light in the room was on but the bed was empty. Her heart thudded in her chest and her throat felt parched.

Suddenly a thought flashed across her mind. What if this crazy young man was the thug's crony?!

She leapt frenziedly towards the safe beside her bed and pulled its handle. It was locked. But then she remembered—she kept the key of the safe beneath the pillow… Once again she was short of breath.

She turned the pillow over. The key of the safe was lying there. But Roshi was not satisfied. She opened the safe. Her nervousness gradually subsided. All her valuables and money were intact.

But where did he go then? Closing the safe she stood straight. She opened the back door. Then she realized—he must have left the room from this door! The door was not locked. It had opened immediately when she had turned the handle! The passageway was dark. She did not dare to step outside. She closed the door and locked it from inside.

Roshi came back to the living room. Why did that idiot leave like this, after all? Her mind raced. Why did he need to run like this? She hadn't brought him here by force. He had come by himself! But why had he come? What was the purpose?

Suddenly she heard someone pounding on the panes of the outside door. She turned back with a start. Meanwhile pieces of glass had shattered onto the floor. Then, through the gap created by the broken glass, a hand entered and searched for the lock—a large, strong-looking hand covered in hair. A faint scream escaped her mouth. But the next moment the hand disappeared and it seemed to Roshi as though two men were pummelling each other outside her door.

A shiver ran down Roshi's spine. She heard a hideous cry after which there was a loud thud, as though something heavy had fallen to the ground.

Then, the sound of running feet.

And now it was utterly silent! Not a single sound could be heard. However, an incessant hissing echoed in Roshi's mind. Her throat was parched and her eyes were burning.

She sat curled up on the sofa, motionless. She did not know what to do. Someone banged on the door after a while, and once again she felt as though her spirit was leaving her body.

'It's me. Open the door,' came a voice from outside. Roshi was not ready to believe her ears—it was the stupid young man's voice.

'Sushi...Sushi...er...Roshi, open the door...! It's me, Imran!'

Roshi leapt to the door. The next moment Imran was standing before her, making faces. He had a few scratches across his face and his lips were bleeding, but he was otherwise unharmed. Roshi pulled him inside quickly and closed the door.

'What happened, where were you?'

'I've retrieved three packets. Two still remain. Well, some other day!' Imran said, throwing three wads of notes on the floor.

'Was it him?' Roshi asked in a fearful voice.

'Yes...he escaped. Two packets are still with him.'

'You are injured. Come to the bathroom,' Roshi said, holding his hand and pulling him to the bathroom.

Soon, they were again sitting on the sofa, staring at each other.

'Why did you go outside?!' Roshi exclaimed.

'I had come to protect you... I knew he'd definitely come! Someone who can fire in the middle of a road—what could prevent him from someone's house?'

'Are you really as stupid as you seem?' Roshi asked in surprise.

'I don't know! I consider myself no less than Plato's grandfather, but others say I am stupid. Let them say what they will; how does it matter? If I am smart, I am smart for myself, and if I am stupid, I am stupid for myself too.'

'So now that unknown man has become my enemy too!' Roshi said, licking her dry lips.

'Of course he will be your enemy too! Why did you try to save my life?!'

'Oh...but...what do I do? Will you protect me forever? No, of course not.'

'He won't dare come here during the day. I'll guard you at night.'

'But how long can this go on...?'

'Until I kill him,' Imran said.

'You...! What the devil are you, after all?'

'I am a devil?' Imran looked upset.

'Oh...dear...you didn't get what I meant.'

'Dear...! I mean, you are calling me *dear*?!' Imran yelled delightfully.

'Yes, of course. What's wrong with that? Aren't we close friends?' Roshi said, smiling.

'No woman has ever called me *dear*!' Imran said in an injured tone of voice.

Chapter 4

SUB-INSPECTOR JAVED OF THE Intelligence Bureau's Shadabnagar branch possessed a redoubtable personality. He was an intelligent young officer. Although he belonged to the Intelligence Bureau his close friends usually called him the prison guard because he laid great emphasis on using his baton to get results. He held that the baton was the best detective on earth. On mere suspicion he'd beat alleged criminals so hard that they would confess crimes they could never even imagine committing. He was a large, strongly built man. In fact, several of the alleged criminals would accept their crimes as soon as they saw him! But even he had been unable to get a glimpse of the criminal of Shadabnagar who had driven to despair the citizens who lived by the port.

At this moment Sub-Inspector Javed was sitting in his superintendent's office, waiting for the superintendent to finish his work and notice his presence. The superintendent was scribbling on a piece of paper. After a while, he put his pen down and stretched his arms. He smiled when he saw Javed.

'So I have called you here to tell you that you'll have to assist Imran Sahib. Alas, because of our sheer helplessness in this case we've had to seek assistance from the Central Office!'

'Imran Sahib?' Javed said, astonished. 'The one famous for the Li Yu Ka case?'

'Yes...yes,' the superintendent said, nodding. 'That sire arrived here the day before yesterday but he hasn't reported here yet. These Central Office people are very shrewd; be careful lest our department is discredited. From amongst my men I couldn't think of anyone more capable than you.'

'Please don't worry—I'll do my best.'

'Refrain from taking initiatives yourself, just follow his lead.'

'I will make sure of that.'

The phone rang and the superintendent picked up the receiver.

'Hello... Oh, it's you! Yes...yes...okay...wait...just a second.'

The superintendent grabbed a pencil and started scribbling in his diary. He was still holding the receiver to his ear.

After some time he said, 'So when are you meeting us...yes...okay, okay, I'll make sure of that.' He placed the receiver on the hook, leaned back in his chair, and was lost in thought.

'Look, Javed,' he said after a while. 'Imran Sahib just called! He has given us serial numbers of a few counterfeit currency notes, and has asked us to monitor them. He wants anyone with these notes to be arrested immediately. Note down these numbers. But I have no idea what all this means!'

'When will he come here?' Javed asked.

'According to him, at one minute and thirty seconds past one. I don't understand what kind of a person he is. But I've heard that he is an Officer on Special Duty and that he has his own section which reports to the Director General directly.'

'I have heard that his father is the Director General?'

'Yes, that's true. But what is this absurdity...one minute and thirty seconds past one!'

Chapter 5

IMRAN WAS WALKING ABOUT the railway station. He was waiting for his subordinate Hoopoe—Hoopoe who stammered, and who was fond of using grandiloquent words in his speech.

The train arrived…and left…but Hoopoe was nowhere to be seen. Imran went to the gate and stood there, scanning the crowd. There was a huge crowd but, finally, after much effort, he managed to locate Hoopoe.

'Come here!' Imran said, gripping his arm and almost dragging him towards the waiting room.

When they reached the waiting room Hoopoe said, 'I-i-i had…luh-luh-lost…my puh-puh-pre-presence…of muh-mind before! Therefore I present you my humble regards now.' He greeted Imran very deferentially by making a low bow.

'May you live long,' Imran said, giving him his blessings. 'Are you familiar with this city?'

'Yes, uh-of course…this is muh-my agnatic cousin's autochthonous land.'

'I don't have time or I would have asked you the meanings of agnatic cousin and autochthonous land! Anyway, you are here to fish.'

'Huh?' Hoopoe said, widening his eyes in astonishment. 'Muh-my buh-bub-br-brain...coh-coh-couldn't reh-register what th-th-that means!'

'You will fish here in the port area. You will stay at the ABC Hotel. Get fishing accessories from the market and go there without any questions. Go...fish!'

'Excuse me, but this is impossible for me.'

'Why is it impossible?' Imran frowned at him.

'My dearest father's will...he states... *La pêche est l'activité de gens inutiles...*'

'What does that mean? I don't know German!'

'Ee-ee-it's fuh-fuh-French, sir. It means that fishing is the activity of useless people.'

'Okay, let me dismiss you from work right now so that you can fish peacefully.'

'Oho...huh-how sh-sh-should I...ex-explain to you!' Hoopoe said.

In an attempt to explain himself to Imran he stammered helplessly for a bit. Imran was in no particular hurry; otherwise he would not have wasted his time in this manner.

'Okay, now go,' he said, pushing him to the door. 'This is official, state work. I'll tell you more when necessary. Don't forget, the ABC Hotel is in the port area. You have to stay there. The fishing spot is not far from there. But beware...never go there in the evening after seven.'

Hoopoe thought for a while, and then said, 'Okay, sir. I am going... Buh-but...I doh-don't know wh-what I w-will ne-need to buh-buy for fishing.'

Imran gave him a detailed account of the accessories he needed to acquire.

Chapter 6

It was exactly one minute and thirty seconds past one when Imran entered the superintendent's office. The superintendent blinked his eyes rapidly in disbelief when he saw a man in the prime of his youth entering the office.

'Please sit down, please sit down,' he said.

'Thank you,' Imran said, sitting down. He did not look like a fool today. He looked like an efficient man with a charismatic personality.

'You made us wait for quite a while,' the superintendent said, extending a packet of cigarettes to him.

'Thank you. I don't smoke,' Imran said. 'The reason I am late is that I have been occupied in assessing the situation.'

'I knew it!' The superintendent laughed.

'Any news on the currency notes?'

'We don't have any news yet, but…'

'You want to know about them,' Imran said smiling.

'Yes! I am curious about them.'

'That person has two wads of counterfeit notes and he has acquired them from me.'

'From you?!' The superintendent's eyes widened in astonishment.

'Yes. I intentionally went to that dangerous area yesterday. And I had wads of counterfeit notes in my pockets.'

'Oh, so the news in today's papers was about you?'

'Perhaps.'

'But it was a dangerous step.'

'Yes! But then sometimes one cannot do without them... But I've changed my mind after the encounter with him. Those counterfeit notes won't come into the market. I informed you about them just to be on the safe side. He is very clever and these kinds of tactics won't work with him.'

The superintendent looked at Imran silently.

'The question is, why does the area become dangerous at night?' Imran murmured. 'Of course, there is an official signboard on the road warning people about the danger and so the route generally remains closed. Still a chance visitor like me was attacked... This means that man reigns over that place all night.'

'Yes, of course. That's completely true, and that is exactly why a warning signboard has been put up there.'

'But the purpose, sir? After all, what is there in that wilderness? If we say that wilderness is a haven for pillagers then one has to wonder why the ABC Hotel has never been attacked. Thousands of rupees are exchanged in gambling there.'

'We also suspect that the ABC Hotel has some link to him but we haven't been able to find any evidence against them.'

Imran did not say anything. He took out a pack of chewing gum from his pocket, ripped off its wrapper, and offered a piece to the superintendent. Although the superintendent accepted it and thanked him, he was obviously baffled. Flushing with embarrassment, and wishing to be rid of Imran, he began to look in every other direction but his.

On the other hand, Imran sat there, comfortably chewing gum. After a while he said, 'I would appreciate it if you keep the story to yourself.'

'Of course,' the superintendent said. Avoiding Imran's gaze, he popped the chewing gum in one of the drawers of his table.

'Where are you staying?' he asked Imran.

'I am staying in some hotel,' Imran replied.

The superintendent did not think it appropriate to enquire further.

Some minutes passed in silence. Then the superintendent said, 'I have chosen someone to assist you. If you like, I can introduce him to you now?'

'No, there is no need right now. You can give me his name and contact information—preferably a number at which he is available all the time. But I will try to not bother you too much.'

The last sentence had perhaps offended the superintendent. His face reddened. But he said nothing.

Imran fidgeted restlessly for a while. Then, extending his hand to the superintendent, he said, 'Okay, thank you very much.'

'Oh...okay. But I would be pleased if you dine with me tonight.'

'I will definitely dine with you,' Imran said, smiling, 'but not today. By the way, I will really need your cooperation.'

'Don't worry about that.'

'Okay, I shall take my leave.' Imran left the room. The superintendent sat silently, shaking his head for a while. Then he pulled open the drawer of his table and took out the gum Imran had given him, and after carefully looking around, popped it into his mouth.

Chapter 7

IMRAN REACHED ROSHI'S FLAT at seven. She was waiting for him. Seeing Imran, she made a face and said irritably, 'You've been gone since this morning! You return now?! I waited for you at lunch; I waited in the evening for tea. It's been a while now!'

'I was looking for your flat in a building on another road,' Imran said, scratching his head.

'Where were you all day?!'

'I kept looking for that wretch from whom I still need to recover two packets!'

'Don't put your life in danger! How do I make you understand?!'

'I am sure he visits ABC Hotel.'

'You won't stop your nonsense?!' Roshi said, standing and shaking him furiously. 'Why didn't you bring your luggage from the hotel?'

'Luggage...oh, forget it...let's go for a walk!'

'I haven't even stepped outside today,' Roshi said.

'Why?'

'I am afraid.'

Imran began to laugh. He said, 'He seems to be the king of the night, not of the day.'

'Whatever it is, but...' Roshi stopped in the middle of the sentence. She turned back and looked fearfully at the door, and said in a low voice, 'Lock the door!'

'Oho! You are so timid.' Imran began laughing again.

'Please close it! I'll tell you something important.'

Imran closed the door and locked it.

Roshi reached into her blouse through the neckline and took out an envelope. Handing it to Imran she said, 'A man came around at three today. He fled before I could open the envelope.'

Imran took out the letter from the envelope. It was in Roman script.

Roshi,
You wouldn't know me, but I am well acquainted with you. If you want to ensure your safety, then tell me everything about the person you were with last night. Who is he? Where has he come from? Why is he here? You can give me all this information on the phone. My phone number is six naught. I will forgive you.

Terror.

'Aha, wonderful,' Imran said, 'so he wants to talk to you on the phone.'

'But wait! I searched through the whole of the telephone directory, and I couldn't locate his number.'

'Do you have a directory?'

'No. But the neighbours have one. They also have a phone.'

'Okay, get the directory,' Imran said.

'You have to come along!'

'Oh, okay...let's go.'

They opened the door and came out. Roshi went into the neighbour's flat while Imran waited outside.

Roshi came out in about five minutes.

Getting back into the flat, she closed the door very carefully behind her. They began searching for six naught in the directory. But they couldn't find it anywhere.

'I think this is nonsense,' Roshi said. 'It is quite possible that someone else sent me this letter just to scare me.'

'But who else is aware of these events?'

'Why, there were dozens of men in the hotel when you were attacked. And then you brought me to the hotel on your shoulders! And then you had also gone to the casino from my table.'

Imran was silent. He was lost in thought. After a while he said, 'We shall now have dinner at a fantabulous restaurant.'

'That's insane! No, we won't go anywhere right now,' Roshi said sternly.

'You'll have to come,' Imran said, 'otherwise I won't be able to sleep all night.'

'Why won't you be able to sleep?'

'Oh... nothing,' Imran said seriously. 'I will just be tormented by the thought that you don't think I am a close friend, and that's why you don't listen to anything I say!'

Roshi stared at him thoughtfully.

'Will it really torment you?' she said softly.

'Whenever any wish of mine is not granted, I feel like crying my eyes out,' Imran said guilelessly.

Roshi stared at him. Imran now had an innocent but foolish expression on his face.

'Okay, I'll come!' Roshi said softly and Imran's eyes gleamed like those of a child given a new toy.

After a while Roshi emerged from her room dressed up. She looked expectantly at Imran, in anticipation of a compliment from him.

Imran made a sour face and said, 'I can apply make-up better than you can!'

'You?'

'Yes, why not? Well, some other time. Shall we leave now?'

'You tease me for no reason,' Roshi said, annoyed.

'Alas, you don't understand Urdu. Otherwise I would have said,

Unko aata hai pyar par gussa
hum hi kar baithay thay Ghalib pesh-dasti
aik din!

She is enraged when I express my love,
Alas! Ghalib...that I made haste one day!

'Come, stop talking nonsense!' she said, pushing Imran to the door.

Roshi was actually looking beautiful! Once outside, Imran hailed a cab and they left for White Marble, the largest and most splendid restaurant of the city.

'Roshi, why don't *I* call him?' Imran said.

'But did we find the number in the directory? No, dear, I think someone was playing a prank on me.'

'I don't think so.'

'Since when are you capable of thinking anything? It is better that you don't think anything at all.'

'Well, I suggest that you dial six naught. If you don't get through, then as a punishment pull off your ears... I mean, my ears.'

'But what will I say?!'

'Listen. Let's call him from a public phone booth on our way. You tell him that the madman is some aristocrat's son who has come from abroad. Say that he got into some trouble today—he received some counterfeit notes by mistake and was caught using them. Saved himself by bribing someone.'

'Counterfeit notes?' Roshi said anxiously.

'Yes, Roshi, that's true,' Imran said, distressed. 'I narrowly escaped disaster today; otherwise I'd have been in jail! Some counterfeit notes have been mixed in my money. I don't know where they came from.'

'They might have been in the packets you snatched from him last night.'

'I don't know,' Imran said, shaking his head dejectedly. 'I made a big blunder; I mixed those notes with the real money!'

'Why don't you tell me the truth? Who are you?' Roshi cried. She was angry now.

'I have told you everything, Roshi!'

'So you are really an idiot!'

'You humiliate me all the time!' Imran was furious.

'Oho, no! No!' Roshi said, rumpling his hair. 'Okay, so what's the story of these counterfeit notes?'

'I think the girl who met me in the railway station's waiting room did this! She replaced genuine notes with fake ones and then invited me to the ABC Hotel! I can guarantee she is that scoundrel's agent. And those wads of notes that I snatched last night—I think I did not really snatch them, but that, in fact, he gave them to me himself! Do you know what that means? The wads he still has with him are the ones with genuine notes, which means that he has taken genuine notes from me and given me counterfeit ones!'

'And those notes...which you lost in gambling?' Roshi asked.

'I cannot say anything about those either. Perhaps they were counterfeit... Or I might have given a wad or a half of genuine notes. Genuine and fake notes are now all mixed up. I don't have the courage to use any of those notes.'

'But how would that girl have stolen all your notes?'

'Oh...' Imran said painfully. 'I am a very unfortunate person. In fact, now I'm convinced that I am an idiot as well... You are right! Yes, so it was a little cold yesterday morning, you know... I was wearing a long overcoat and had stuffed about fifteen to twenty wads in its pockets.'

'You seem to be much more than an idiot!' Roshi said, annoyed.

'No. At least listen to me! I thought I was being really smart! Once, my uncle was travelling. He had fifteen thousand rupees which he kept safely in a suitcase. The suitcase disappeared somewhere on the way! From that day on, it has become my habit to keep all my money on my person when travelling. I haven't been cheated like this before. This is the first blow.'

'But how did that girl con you after all?'

'Don't ask me. I am a complete ass.'

'I know that for a fact. But tell me.'

'Oho, she made an ass out of me! She said, "You greatly resemble my friend who died in an accident last year! And I loved him a lot!" Then within fifteen minutes we were like old friends... I was a little hesitant. She said, "Are you feeling unwell?" I said I had a headache, so she said "Come, let me do some champi for you"...Do you know what champi is?'

'No, I don't.'

Imran began massaging her head like a trained masseuse.

'Stop it, you are messing my hair,' Roshi said, jerking his hand away.

'So she kept massaging my head and I went off to sleep in the comfortable chair of the waiting room. I woke up about half an hour later... She was still massaging my head. To tell you the truth, I really liked her at that time and I wanted her to massage my head like this forever. Ah!... She promised to meet me at the ABC Hotel before leaving me for good.'

Imran's voice quavered. It seemed as if he was about to cry.

'Oho, stupid, you are crying for that woman who robbed you?' Roshi laughed.

'Oh, am I crying?' Imran said, slapping his cheeks. 'No, I am angry! I will strangle her to death.'

'Calm down, my lion, calm down,' Roshi said, patting his shoulder.

'Now you are making fun of me.' Imran was angry.

'No, I sympathize with you. But I was thinking that if you lost counterfeit money while gambling at the hotel casino, then I'll be banned from there too! I won't be surprised if I too am punished for that.'

'No, don't you worry. No one can do you any harm. I'll spend millions of rupees to protect you.'

Roshi did not say anything. She was lost in thought.

'I think there is a telephone booth here,' Imran interjected and asked the driver to stop the car.

The taxi stopped. Roshi and Imran stepped out.

The booth was not occupied. Roshi asked Imran once again what she needed to say. Imran repeated what he had said earlier. Roshi inserted a coin into the phone and began dialling. And then an expression of surprise appeared on her face.

She rapidly spat out everything Imran had asked her to say. Then she was silent, listening to what the person at the other end was saying.

'Look!' she said into the mouthpiece after a while. 'I told you everything I know. I don't know anything other than what I've told you! But I do have my doubts about him. He seems to be stupid and crazy.'

'Where has he come from?' the voice on the other end asked.

'He says he has come from Dilawarpur.'

'Is he with you right now?'

'No, he is outside in the taxi. I am calling from a public booth. I have lied to him that I have to deliver a message to a friend.'

'Have you ever met him before last night?'

'No, never,' Roshi replied.

'Did you show him my letter?'

'No...should I?' Roshi asked. But she did not get a response. The line was disconnected from the other end. Roshi replaced the receiver on the hook.

Imran dialled the telephone exchange enquiry number immediately.

'Hello, Enquiry?'

'Hello,' a voice said from the other end.

'Someone's number was dialled from public booth number forty-six. I need the address.'

'Who is this?'

'DSP, City,' Imran said.

'Oh...I think there is a misunderstanding,' the voice on the other end said. 'No call has been made from booth forty-six in the last half hour.'

'Okay, thank you.'

Imran replaced the receiver and they came out of the booth.

'You are the Deputy Superintendent of Police? A DSP?' Roshi laughed.

'If I hadn't said this, he would have never told me anything,' Imran said.

'But what did he tell you?'

'That no call has been made from booth forty-six since half an hour. But Roshi, you were wonderful! You did exactly what I asked you to do.'

'How do you know what he said?'

'I guessed the nature of his questions from your answers.'

'Well, you seem to be stupid only when it comes to girls.'

'No, I'm not. You are stupid!' Imran said, irritated.

'Come...come,' she said, pushing him towards the taxi.

'No! You are teasing me continuously by calling me names!'

But Imran did not dwell on the topic. He had a lot on his mind.

'His voice was also strange,' Roshi said. 'It seemed as if a hungry wolf was howling! But...how is it possible...that the exchange didn't have any clue about the call?'

'Oho, forget it! Why should we be interested in that?' Imran said, with a jerk of his head. 'I want to look for the girl who conned me.'

'No, Imran! This strange matter would be of a lot of interest to the police.'

'What matter?'

'That six naught is dialled, a proper call is made, and the exchange doesn't have a clue about it.'

'Oh Roshi, don't! Don't! Don't mention it to anyone! Do you really want to get killed?! If this information reaches the police, then be sure that we'll both be finished. He doesn't seem to be some common thief or purse snatcher... Yes, I've read hundreds of detective novels! In one of them I read that a big criminal had set up his private telephone exchange and the public exchange had no clue about it!'

'So are you afraid of him now?'

'No, I'm not afraid! But how do I tell you, Roshi... I read in that novel that the person was omnipresent! You take his name and he materializes right there... May God protect us!' Imran began slapping his face. Roshi burst out laughing, guffawing for quite a while. Then suddenly she sat up with a start and looked around in astonishment.

'Are you in your senses or not?' she exclaimed in a low voice, leaning towards Imran. 'We are not in the city!'

Widening his eyes Imran looked around himself...The car was moving on a dark, deserted road, and plains and fields stretched far and wide on both sides.

'Dear driver, stop the car,' Imran said to the driver. Almost instantly he heard the loud noise of glass shattering behind him and felt something cold pressed to his neck.

'Don't move. Sit quiet!' a voice barked into his ear. 'Or I will drill a hole in your neck! And girl, you move to the other side.'

The car was an old model, where the trunk lid was hinged at the bottom and opened up from the top, adjacent to the rear window. The man had probably been hiding in the trunk from the very beginning. When the cab reached this quiet spot he'd yanked open the trunk, broken the rear window, and was now pressing a revolver to Imran's neck.

Roshi looked fearfully at the large, broad hand firmly holding the revolver.

Imran did not move an inch. He looked as insensible and motionless as a stone statue. He wasn't even blinking his eyes.

The car was still rushing along. Roshi was getting dizzy. She felt as though the car was moving towards an abyss... Her eyes drooped shut.

Suddenly she heard a scream close to her ear...and her eyes snapped open in shock. Imran was staring into the darkness through the gap in the rear screen, and he had the revolver in his hand.

'Driver, stop the car!' Imran said, pointing the revolver at him.

The driver did not even turn his head.

'I am talking to you!' This time he struck the driver's head with the revolver's butt. The driver swore and turned around, but was stunned to see the revolver pointed at him.

'Stop the car, dear,' Imran said softly. 'Your partner's spine must be broken because the car was speeding.'

The car halted.

'Good,' Imran continued softly. 'So now, will you listen to Raga Bhairavi, the raga of terror, or would you like to listen to durgat,[1] or whatever you call it... It's called dhrupat, I think, but the educated usually call it dhrupad.'

The driver did not utter a word. He was licking his dry lips.

'Roshi! Undo his tie,' Imran said.

---

[1] A play on words. Durgat, which sounds similar to the name of a classical long-term called Dhrupad, means the act of beating.

Chapter 8

Roshi and Imran were driving back to the city. Imran was on the steering. The driver was lying helpless on the back seat. Imran had secured his hands behind his back with his tie, and had used his belt to tie his legs. Imran had also stuffed two handkerchiefs into his mouth to prevent him from screaming.

Below the seat was a corpse with a smashed face. Black curtains had been drawn over the windows.

Roshi sat in petrified silence. She had been trying to say something for quite a while but was unable to find her voice. But how long could she keep quiet? The corpse in the car made her want to scream wildly.

'I think you should now go straight to the police station,' Roshi said.

'Oh, my, my!' Imran murmured.

'You'll have to go! It's nothing...it's nothing to worry about! Whatever we tell them won't be wrong. You killed him in self-defence!'

'That's all fine...but police trouble...! No, I can't handle that.'

'Then what will become of the corpse?! Why did you pick it up from there?! You should have left the driver there as well! We would have left the car outside the city and walked back!'

'Why didn't you bless me with this advice at that time?!' Imran said angrily. 'What can we do now? We are already in the city.'

Roshi felt completely drained. She wiped sweat from her brow and said, 'We still have a chance, let's go back.'

'You seem to be more stupid than I am! If we encounter five or ten of them this time, they'll turn me into an omelette and you into custard.'

'Then what will you do?'

'Let's see. I am on to something. But I won't tell you what it is! You will again give me advice that will insult my intelligence.'

Roshi was silent. Not because she didn't have an answer but because her body was trembling terribly and her throat was parched.

Imran took the car to a locality which housed rental garages.

He stopped the car in front of a garage, stepped out, and began negotiating the rent of the garage. He told the garage manager that he was a tourist staying at the Coronation Hotel, but since no parking space was available there he needed to rent a garage. It wasn't something unusual so it didn't prove difficult to get a garage.

He paid for a week in advance, and obtained the receipt and the keys of the garage. Then, locking the car in the garage, he walked with Roshi until they came to another road.

'But what will happen now?' Roshi murmured.

'That driver too will die by tomorrow morning,' Imran replied very simply.

'You are a complete ass.' Roshi was annoyed.

'No, I am not that stupid. I didn't give him my correct name and address.'

'Don't count on that,' Roshi said bitterly. 'The police will chase you like hounds.'

'Don't worry! No one will open that garage for a week since I have paid a week's rent in advance. And in one week—who knows where I'll be...! I might even be dead... Or that rogue may die... Anyway, he has lost two of his men.'

Roshi did not reply. Her head was spinning.

Imran stopped a passing cab, opened the door for Roshi, got in himself, and said to the driver, 'White Marble.'

Roshi stared at him wide-eyed.

'Yes,' Imran said, nodding. 'We'll eat there. Have coffee. And you can drink a peg or two. You'll feel better. By the way, if you like chewing gum I can give you some... And yes, we will also dance a round or two of rumba!'

'Are you really crazy?' Roshi said softly.

'Huh? Sometimes you call me stupid, sometimes you call me mad! I will now strangle myself!'

Roshi was silent. She had much to say in this regard but she couldn't find the words. She was extremely flustered. She felt like running home screaming like a madwoman.

They reached the White Marble. Imran sat her in a cabin and went to the restroom. But that was just an excuse. He actually wanted to go to the cabin that had the payphone. He dialled the number on which Inspector Javed was available all the time.

'Hello...who is this? I would like to talk to Inspector Javed... Oh it's you. Ali Imran speaking... Yes... Look, in garage number thirteen at Amir Ganj, which is locked, you'll find a blue car. There are two quarries in it. One is dead. You might find the other alive. I have the keys to the garage. Take a search warrant and break the lock without hesitation. Yes, yes...it is related to the same matter... I'm sure that both of them are his men! And listen, we need to be very secretive. This incident should remain a secret! You'll get all the details tomorrow morning. Okay, goodnight.'

Imran replaced the receiver and returned to Roshi.

Roshi was in a terrible state. Imran ordered sherry for her. This had a positive effect on her—she seemed a little rejuvenated. But she still could not bring herself to eat anything. She looked at Imran in astonishment. He had pounced on the food as though he had not eaten for days, and that old foolish expression had appeared on his face again.

'You are very quiet,' Imran said to Roshi, without raising his head.

'Nothing...nothing in particular,' Roshi said dejectedly.

'What about rumba? I am in the mood to dance.'

'Don't bother me, for God's sake!'

'Are you a woman or... Tell me, should I have died at their hands?! They would have taken us somewhere and made mincemeat of us!'

'I don't want to talk about it,' Roshi said, rubbing her forehead.

'I didn't want to talk either! First you prod me and then react as though you are going to eat me alive!'

'Imran dear...just think, what will happen now?'

'The second one will die too... And when after three days the rotting bodies reek, they will be compelled to break the garage's lock. And then the owner of the car will be arrested. Haha.'

'And what about the fact that you showed them your face?' Roshi said angrily.

'To the garage people?' Imran asked.

Roshi nodded.

'But they didn't see you! So you are safe!' Imran said.

'I am concerned about you!' Roshi snapped.

'Don't worry about me... I am a Pathan. I won't leave this city until I finish that scoundrel! By the way, I cannot stay with you any more.'

'Why?' Roshi stared at him.

'You humiliate me every other instant. Idiot... crazy—God knows what you call me all the time. You get annoyed and then you annoy me...'

Roshi smiled slightly.

'You will dance the rumba with me!' Imran said, stressing each word.

'Hmm. Okay,' Roshi said, standing up. 'Let's go, but remember this...you are really stressing me out!'

The two of them entered the dance hall. Numerous couples were dancing. Soon, Imran and Roshi had disappeared into the crowd.

Chapter 9

THE NEXT DAY IMRAN was sitting in the superintendent's office at the Intelligence Bureau.

He sported a thick beard which conferred upon him a pious air, so much so that he looked like a kind-hearted padre. When he had entered the room, he'd also been wearing dark glasses which he had now taken off.

The superintendent was reading the report which Imran had compiled about the previous night's incidents.

'But, sir,' the superintendent said after a while, 'that's a stolen car! A complaint about its theft was lodged in the police station last week.'

'That's fine,' Imran said, nodding. 'Such cars are generally used in these kinds of activities. I am assuming that car theft is a regular occurrence here?'

'You are right about that. But then we find the cars parked somewhere! This is the first time a man has been caught along with such a car.'

'What information did you get from the driver?' Imran asked.

'Nothing. He says that he was hired yesterday evening. Actually he is a taxi driver and he was offered three hundred rupees for three hours of work.'

'Ahem. So this means that the person who could have told us anything is dead... Anyway... But can we at least investigate the identity of the deceased? Where did he live? What circles did he move in?'

'Javed is working on that and I am confident that he will make good progress.'

'Right. Okay, do you know whether...but no... Anyway, what was I saying just now?'

Imran became silent and began drumming his forehead with his fingers. Actually he was about to tell the superintendent about the phone number six naught—but then he thought of something, and stopped.

'Ah, I've forgotten that too!' Imran said gravely. Suddenly, he seemed to be struck by some profound grief; he heaved a deep sigh, and in a despondent tone, said, 'I don't know if it's some temporary ailment or some mental disease... Suddenly I lose track of my thoughts and I forget everything. Anyway, I might remember it later. I was going to tell you something.'

The superintendent looked at him curiously. But it was not easy to judge from Imran's face what he really felt.

They talked about different aspects of the case for a bit. The superintendent told him that three men of the ABC Hotel had been caught using counterfeit money. Imran asked for the serial numbers of those notes. The superintendent removed a list from his drawer and handed it to Imran.

'No,' Imran said, shaking his head. 'These are only from amongst the notes I lost in the hotel. I don't see any notes from the packets that were stolen by the unknown marauder.'

'Then we will have to admit that the people at the ABC Hotel have nothing to do with this man. Of course if he had any idea that we were tracking notes he would have stopped the ABC people from using them.'

'No, we can't say anything conclusive about that,' Imran said. 'It is possible that he might have handed those ABC people to the police on purpose... You know, to fool us into believing that he has no connection with them.'

'Yes, that's possible too.' The superintendent nodded.

'We should ignore the ABC staff for the moment,' Imran said.

'But what will you do now?' the superintendent asked.

'It's difficult to say. I never begin with a strategy in mind. I do whatever occurs to me at that instant. Let's see how he reacts to last night's incident. I am waiting for his reaction.'

Imran left soon after. A new idea had sprung to his mind. After leaving the superintendent's office, he began to walk briskly, simultaneously keeping an eye out for anyone who might be following him.

He hadn't mentioned Roshi to the superintendent. He wanted to keep her behind the scenes.

After walking for a short distance he stopped at a telephone booth. He turned to look around; not a soul was in sight. It wasn't a busy road. A car or two would go by occasionally, or a pedestrian would walk by.

Imran opened the door of the booth and entered. After locking it from the inside he put half a quarter in the slot and dialled six naught.

'Hello,' a heavy voice said from the other side.

'This is Roshi,' Imran said into the mouthpiece in a woman's voice. If Roshi were present here right now, she would have definitely fainted from shock.

'Roshi?'

'Yes, I am very worried.'

'Why?'

'He killed a man last night... The man was hiding in the trunk of our car. Then at one point the man broke through the rear windscreen and pointed a revolver at us. I don't know how he threw the man overboard,' Imran said, recounting the entire episode. 'I was very worried. I asked him to inform the police but he refused... I didn't know what to do. Anyway, I called the police in my anxiety and told them that there is a corpse in a particular garage. But I didn't disclose my identity.'

'Does he know that you called the police?'

'No. I didn't tell him. I am very anxious. He seems to be a very dangerous man... But I don't know who he is.'

'Where are you speaking from right now?'

'I won't tell you. I'm afraid of you too!'

The person at the other end laughed softly and said, 'You are calling from public booth number twenty-four.'

Imran's eyes widened with astonishment.

'I am going,' he said nervously.

'No, wait! It's safer for you to just stay there... You know what will happen otherwise? What if the police catch you? I have no quarrel with you; in fact, you have inadvertently helped me on several occasions. I want to save you from this mess... Yes, so I was saying that you stay outside the booth—one of my men will be there within half an hour.'

'Why...no, no,' Imran said, protesting. 'I am completely innocent. What do I do?! He has become a pain in my neck for no reason!'

'Don't fear me, Roshi,' the person said, making kissing sounds. 'I want to help you. Your safety lies in listening to me.'

Imran did not reply immediately.

'Hello,' the voice said.

'Hello,' Imran said in a quavering voice. 'Okay, I'll wait but I'm sure this is the last day of my life!'

'You are terrified,' the person said, laughing. 'Well, if I wanted to kill you, you wouldn't have been alive today! Okay then, wait there.'

The call was disconnected immediately.

Imran came out of the booth. He had a smirk on his lips. And God knows why that smile looked terrifying with that beard.

He had to wait for half an hour. He crossed over to the other side of the road. There were a few shady trees on this side.

Last night he had already taken care of Roshi's safety. At the moment she was staying at an obscure hotel and Imran had spent the night alone in her flat.

He paced up and down under the trees while glancing at his wristwatch every few minutes. Twenty minutes passed in this manner. He walked to the booth once again.

Soon he heard a car stop behind him.

Suddenly Imran had a coughing fit. Pressing his stomach, he bent forward and began coughing violently. Then, straightening up, he waved his fist in the direction of the booth and said angrily, 'Goddamn it! Where will you go? You will have to come out of the booth at some point!'

'What is it, sir?' a voice behind him asked.

Imran turned around with a start. A handsome young man stood by a car that was parked a few feet away.

'What can I say, sir!' Imran said, panting heavily as though the cough attack had left him breathless. After a few gasps he said, 'She has been in that booth for the past one hour. I have to make an important call too... I have knocked several times, but to no avail! She just says "wait a minute" and doesn't leave. A minute, she says?! Dammit, it has been a whole hour!'

'Oh, wait. Let me have a look,' the young man said, walking towards the booth. He opened the door, and before he had a chance to turn around and interrogate Imran, Imran grabbed his neck. He shoved him into the booth and pummelled him to the ground.

The booth's door was automatic so Imran did not need to bother about latching it; as soon as they had entered, it closed by itself with a soft click.

Slaps, punches, and kicks were accompanied by a stream of invective. Imran said, 'I am Roshi. I am beating the hell out of you, my love. Tell your Bulldog that he has to return my money or else I'll lock him in a mousetrap and beat the hell out of him too... And that Roshi! She tricked me too! I haven't seen her since last night. She has disappeared! And, kiddo, you know that last night I broke one of your comrades' back, right?!'

Imran had pounced upon the man so suddenly that he hadn't had a chance to process a thing. He had no choice but to get a sound thrashing. He stopped resisting after a while.

Imran picked him up by his collar but his legs wouldn't support his weight.

'Look, kid. Tell your Bulldog that I better get my money tonight or else... Those notes are counterfeit! I didn't want to bring them into the market yet! But my game has been ruined because of that dog! Who is he to meddle in the affairs of others? Tell him that I better get the notes tonight. I will be at Roshi's place. She has fled somewhere out of fear... Tonight! Don't forget! I will be in Roshi's flat! And tell that cowardly pickpocket that a police officer is staying at the ABC Hotel on the pretext of nabbing some fish. Be cautious.'

The he yanked him out of the booth.

The road was deserted. The young man could easily have settled the score in the open space, but the truth was that he did not have any strength for such a strenuous undertaking.

Imran plopped him before the steering wheel.

'Go, now get lost,' Imran said. 'Otherwise it is quite possible that I may treat you to some more special care. Do deliver my message to your Bulldog! Otherwise you know what will happen, right? Wherever I find you, in darkness or in light, I will whisk you into an omelette!'

Chapter 10

IMRAN HAD TRIED TO shape Hoopoe into someone much like himself. Hoopoe was a bit stupid, but Imran's slightest command could spur him into action. Sluggish and slow otherwise, he was very efficient when it came to work.

But he was extremely frustrated by the job Imran had given him today. He could have even tolerated the work, but he was loath to stay at the ABC Hotel. But then he feared Imran. The poor guy was still unaware of what he was actually supposed to do—the Bureau did not pay him to go fishing after all!

He had shifted into a room at the hotel yesterday, and today, according to Imran's instructions, he was supposed to fish at the coast from morning until night. But he was disgusted with the atmosphere of the ABC Hotel, where he had to continuously suffer the company of immoral men and women.

At the moment he was sitting at the breakfast table and gulping down a cup of tea. He intended to escape as soon as possible. He had spotted, standing by the counter, the woman who had greatly bothered him last night. She had been very drunk and had pestered him to sing her the song *'Baalam aan baso morey mann main'* (O my love come dwell in my heart) from the movie *Devdas*. His discomfiture had been palpable and people around had looked on in amusement. God alone knows how he had escaped her clutches.

Seeing her again, he began twitching nervously. But the woman wasn't drunk any more. In fact, she looked quite serious. He rapidly finished his breakfast, grabbed his fishing equipment from his room, and left for the wharf.

Hoopoe was aware that they had come to this place on a mission. But he had no idea what he was supposed to do at the wharf. At any rate he decided it was best to keep his eyes open and watch out for trouble.

The sea was calm. Launches and boats did not frequent this area. He saw a few other men on the wharf who were dozing with their fishing gear set up.

He tried some angling until one o'clock, but not a single fish took the bait.

But, intent on nabbing fish, perhaps he was unaware of the fact that a man was lurking nearby to nab him.

That man puffed on a cigarette for a while. Then he slowly moved towards Hoopoe.

'It's difficult to get a catch these days,' he said, sitting at a short distance from Hoopoe.

Hoopoe looked at him with a start. He was a tall, slim man in his thirties. A camera was slung on his shoulder.

'Ye-yes!' Hoopoe said, trying to be polite.

'What do you think of this hobby?' the young man asked.

'Puh-puh-pardon me. I di-di-didn't understand.'

'Oh... I hope you don't misunderstand me. Actually I work for an illustrated monthly. And it is my job to provide information and photographs about different hobbies.'

'This isn't my hobby... it's my puh-puh-profession,' Hoopoe said, smiling.

'I can't believe that, sir.' The young man laughed. 'The professionals here use large fishing nets. And they don't wear such fancy clothes. Nor do they wear straw hats.'

Hoopoe began giggling for no apparent reason.

The young man said, 'I shall be grateful to you if you pose for me with your fishing equipment.'

'I am not the oh-oh-only one here.'

'That's correct. But I don't consider the others worthy of a photograph. After all this photo will be published in a monthly that is circulated in the US, England, France, Germany, Holland, and other such countries!'

Hoopoe pumped up his chest like a proud rooster and posed for three photos. But he stuttered badly when it came to expressing his views on the hobby. Of course, the only things he knew about fish were that all fish are not equally delicious, and that no matter which class a fish belongs to, it will definitely have bones.

'I ca-ca-cannot...tell you vuh-vuh-verbally,' he said at last, frustrated. 'I can...gi-give it to you in writing.'

'It happens...it happens,' the young man said, nodding. 'Some people can write but cannot speak.

Anyway, that's no problem. Whatever I know about fishing, I will add that myself. But do give me your name and contact information.'

Hoopoe heaved a sigh of relief. Of course, he must have given a fake name and address. The young man departed. But someone was lying in wait for this young man as well. As soon as the young man crossed the sandy area and reached the road leading to the port, a man emerged from behind a mound and began following him. This man was none other than Imran.

Chapter 11

Roshi had been waiting for Imran at her hotel since last night. After getting her a room in the hotel Imran had left, promising her that he would return shortly. She was very worried about him. But she did not have the courage to go out and search for him.

She was also afraid of the police. And that terrifying man was after her already.

The day was over but Imran hadn't returned. It was four in the evening and Roshi had lost all hope. She was sure that Imran was in deep trouble. Either the police had got their hands on him, or that terrifying man. She trembled at the thought. She imagined Imran dead.

She shifted restlessly on her bed. She did not know what to do. Suddenly someone knocked at the door. Roshi jumped, but then she thought that it must be room service since it was time for tea.

'Come in,' Roshi said dejectedly.

The door opened. Imran was standing before her, smiling.

'You!' Roshi exclaimed, and instantly leaped towards him. 'Where were you?! I'll kill you!'

'What?' Imran stepped back gingerly as though he was actually anticipating an attack.

Roshi began laughing. She shook him hard and said, 'You dirty swine! Tell me, where have you been?!'

'I was looking for Aunt Farzana's house,' Imran said gravely.

'Why? Who is she?'

'I don't know,' Imran said, heaving a sigh. 'I have heard that she knows a person whose left ear has been lopped in half.'

'There you go with your senseless gibberish again! Why did you leave me here like this?'

'Do you want to die?'

'Yes, I want to die!' Roshi said, irritated.

'Okay, then start reading Urdu romantic novels! You'll soon die of boredom.'

'Imran! I'll shoot you.'

'Come, sit down,' Imran said, nudging her into a comfortable chair. 'Both our lives depend on that unknown villain's death.'

Roshi stared at him in silence. Then she said, 'Who the hell are you...tell me! I think I'll go mad!'

'Did you inform the police last night?'

'Inform them about what?' Roshi started.

'That there is a dead body in garage number thirteen.'

'Of course not! Why would I inform them?'

'I don't know. Then who is that woman... Did you see today's evening paper?'

'No, I didn't. Tell me the whole story, don't annoy me.'

'The police have discovered the body after breaking the garage's lock. The driver was alive. He had only fainted. The newspaper reports that some unknown woman, who sounded Anglo-Indian from her accent, informed the police about it over the phone.'

'I'm willing to swear that I said nothing!'

'I'm sure you can never do something like that. What I wanted to say was—don't step outside the hotel without my permission even if you don't see me for a week.'

'I cannot promise that.'

'Why?'

'I'll come with you. You can't leave me here alone.'

'You want both our heads to be chopped off together?'

'I don't know why but I am not afraid of anyone when you are around.'

'Okay, stay here for just one more night.'

'But why? What are you up to? Tell me!'

'No, Roshi, you are very nice. You will stay here tonight. Okay, tell me, have you ever seen someone at the ABC Hotel whose left ear is lopped off?'

Roshi began to blink rapidly as she concentrated hard to remember.

'Why? Why are you asking me this?' she asked softly. 'No, I haven't seen any such man there. But I do know one man who fits the description.'

'Does he belong to the ABC?' Imran asked.

'No. He is not a man of such means. He cannot afford expensive places like the ABC. He works on a fisherman's boat.'

'Are you sure that his left ear is lopped off?'

'Yes! But you...'

'Shh, wait! Tell me. Where can I find him now?'

'How would I know? I don't know where he lives.'

'Then tell me the name of the boat where he works.'

'Hirschfield Fisheries.'

'Hirschfield Fisheries,' Imran repeated, drawing a long breath. Then he stood up and said, 'Okay, tata. I'll see you tomorrow morning.'

'Wait! Tell me what you are up to!'

'I want to retrieve the rest of my money!'

'Whatever it is,' Roshi said, staring at him, 'now you don't appear as foolish to me as you appeared that night at the ABC.'

'You called me a fool again! You yourself are a fool!'

Imran showed her a fist and left the room.

Chapter 12

ROSHI'S FLAT WAS BRIGHTLY lit today. Imran had added a few more lights. He was alone in the flat.

If anyone from the Bureau knew of Imran's activities today, they would have certainly considered him utterly insane. He had been committing apparent blunders all day. Getting hold of one of the criminals and then letting him go after a mild beating was a huge mistake on principle. Imran should have arrested him and then forced him to identify the rest of his aides. Then, Imran had also informed the fellow of Hoopoe's existence. In fact, he had also told him that he would be spending the night at Roshi's flat.

And now he had illuminated the flat as if for some special event. The clock struck twelve and he looked at the doors which were wide open. But he could hear nothing except the ticking of the clock. He had even left the windows wide open tonight despite the biting cold. Suddenly he heard footsteps along the corridor. Then someone softly sang, 'Roshi darling.'

Soon a young man was standing at the door, blinking away like an idiot.

'Yes, please.' Imran smiled warmly.

'Oh...excuse me!' the man said, embarrassed. 'Roshi lived here before.'

'She still lives here. Please come in,' Imran said.

The young man came inside.

'Where is Roshi?'

'She is at her aunt's place these days, learning the art of poultry farming.'

'Who are you?'

'I am a decent person.'

'Roshiii,' the young man called out.

'I'm telling you, she's not here right now,' Imran said.

'Oh, she's very naughty,' the young man said, laughing. 'She has hidden herself somewhere on hearing my voice. Anyway, I'll find her.'

The young man barged into Roshi's bedroom. Imran followed him. The man searched the entire flat within a few minutes, then flashed a torch into the dark corridor at the back of the house.

'Enough, my lad,' Imran said, putting his hand on his shoulder. 'I see you haven't lost your milk teeth yet.'

'What do you mean?' The young man turned angrily.

'I'll tell you what I mean...come with me,' Imran said and brought him to the sitting room. The young man was looking at him angrily.

'Please be seated, sir,' Imran said with exaggerated courtesy.

'What did you just say?' the young man said, annoyed.

'I said that you have searched the place thoroughly. You are sure that there are no other men with me. Now take your leave and tell your Bulldog to return my money. I really am a bad guy. I don't operate a gang. I work alone. I am alone in this flat right now. But I can claim that your Bulldog can't even damage a single hair on my head. See...I have kept all the doors open...and all the lights are on... But, haha...nothing!'

'I don't get what you are saying!'

'Get lost, friend, don't annoy me. Deliver my message to the person who has sent you here. Hurry up and get lost, or I'll end up beating you too. I battered one of your comrades to a pulp just today.'

'I will take care of you!' the young man said. Rising, he rushed out of the room like a whirlwind.

Imran continued standing as though he was still expecting someone to drop in. He took out a pack of chewing gum from his pocket, picked out one, and began chewing it slowly. Seconds turned into minutes, and minutes turned into hours, but he did not hear a single sound.

And then Imran really started feeling like a fool. He had been so sure that the unknown person would come to the flat. But it was two in the morning now, and a deep, still silence reigned over the place.

He thought that he should now end this folly. It was probable that the young man was one of Roshi's clients... Imran got up to close the windows and doors.

He hadn't even reached the door when the sound of feet echoed in the corridor. Someone was approaching very quickly. Imran promptly took a few steps back.

The next instant his eyes widened with astonishment. Roshi was standing at the door and she was panting heavily—but there were no signs of fear on her face.

'You didn't listen to me!' Imran said, scowling.

'You can only talk such nonsense!' Roshi exclaimed, falling into a sofa. Then she opened her handbag, took out two wads of money, and threw them at Imran. She said, 'Here, take your remaining two bundles!'

Imran turned the wads over and over again and then stared at Roshi in astonishment.

'I almost had a heart attack,' Roshi said.

'Why? Where did you get these bundles from?'

'Wait, let me catch my breath!' Roshi said, standing up. She took out a bottle of whisky from a cupboard, poured herself a stiff drink, and began sipping it. Then, wiping her lips with a napkin, she said, 'I wasn't able to sleep. At precisely 1 am someone knocked at my door. I thought it was you. I opened the door. But it was not you, it was someone else. He gave me both these bundles and this envelope...which had my name written on it... And then without giving me a chance to say anything, he quietly went off.'

Roshi removed the envelope from her bag and extended it to Imran.

Imran took out the letter from the envelope, spread it on the table, and drew a deep breath. The letter read,

Roshi, I am sending your friend's two bundles. But you will not untie them. There is a blue car outside the hotel. Seat yourself in it quietly. It will take you to your flat. No matter how much you both try to hide yourselves, you cannot hide from me. I have no problems with either of you. If I did have a problem you wouldn't be alive today. Your friend is a lowly criminal; he runs a business of counterfeit money, and that's all. Tell him to leave the city quietly. You have known me for a long time, so you know what can happen to you! I don't want anything from either of you. Just tell him to leave this city immediately.

Imran finished reading the letter, turned to Roshi, and asked, 'And you sat in the blue car?'

'What else? I thought, now that he knows of my whereabouts why would he hesitate to hurt me?'

'That's fine. You acted wisely.'

'But...' Roshi said, staring at Imran, 'is it true? What he has written about you?'

'He is talking nonsense! How dare he accuse me of this? I will avenge this dishonour!'

'Look, Parrot...I have thought a lot about you...! And yes...why have you illuminated this place? Is someone getting married?'

'I want plenty of light! But you must have thought I was a criminal, what else? Okay, you'll never see me here again.'

'So you really are leaving this city.'

'I am not bound to follow every Tom, Dick, and Harry's orders! And then, do you think I am afraid of that joker? And that I'm going to flee town because of him?'

'For God's sake, who are you?!'

'A lowly criminal. Didn't you believe what he said?'

'No, I didn't believe him. A lowly criminal wouldn't dare to stand against him! The brave warriors of this city tremble when they hear his name. You are well aware of my profession. I rub shoulders with all sorts of men!'

'I am a decent man! Mummy and Daddy have assured me of this fact since I was a child,' Imran said gloomily. 'By the way, sometimes I do really stupid things, like today...!'

Imran recounted the telephone booth episode. Roshi burst into laughter. She said, 'You are a liar! How can you mimic my voice?'

'Like this...what is so difficult about this?' Imran said in Roshi's voice and accent.

Roshi looked at him in astonishment for a while. Then she said, 'But what was the purpose of this?'

'Fun! What else? But look at the result! He returned the bundles himself!'

'You have lost your mind!' Roshi exclaimed. 'I think he is out to trap us.'

'Quite possible... Anyway, I know that his men have been following us for a while now. I mean, there is no other way he could have known your whereabouts, right?'

'That's what I was thinking too!'

'I think it must have been the time when I met you in the evening! He must have followed me to the hotel.'

'But Imran...that man...who brought these bundles...do you know who he was? I am surprised... He was the same fisherman whose left ear is lopped off, the one whom you were asking me about!'

Imran sat up attentively.

'Did he recognize you?' he asked.

'I'm not sure. No, I haven't talked to him before.'

Imran's forehead creased in thought. After a while he stretched his arms and said, 'Go, now go to sleep. I am also sleepy. And any more of your boring stories—I leave.'

Roshi got up quietly and went to her bedroom.

After closing the windows and doors of the flat, Imran ruminatively chewed gum for a while. Then he untied the wads of notes. He knew that something must be hidden in the bundles because Roshi had been instructed in the letter not to untie them.

He was right. He found a letter folded between the notes. It was addressed to Imran.

Friend...you seem to be fearless, and a very shrewd man to boot! But the business of counterfeit money is really low and cheap! If you wish to advance your career meet me at 11 pm tomorrow at the same wilderness where I had attacked you the first time... Thanks for informing me about the spy posted at the ABC Hotel! He is staying there for the sole purpose of fishing, but doesn't know a thing about angling!

I take it that you will meet me tomorrow night...
I will wait.

Imran shredded the letter into tiny pieces and threw them into the fireplace. A devilish smile spread across his face... He got up and quietly left Roshi's flat.

Chapter 13

THE NEXT EVENING IMRAN reached the wilderness where he had been called. It was a dark, moonless night. The ABC Hotel's lights could be seen miles away.

Imran was standing at the same place where he had been attacked a few days ago. He did not have to wait too long.

'So you are here,' he heard a sharp whisper behind him.

Imran turned around with a start. He saw a dark shadow at a short distance.

'Yes, I am,' Imran whispered back. 'And I am not in the least afraid of you.'

'I need a man just like you!' the shadow replied. 'I will make you a millionaire in no time.'

'I don't want to become a millionaire... I have only come because...'

'Stop it! I don't want to hear anything. You are rash and impulsive...still a mere adolescent! You will realize the value of money when you become an old man!'

'What are you trying to imply?' Imran asked.

'Come with me.'

'Let's go. But don't force me to get married! I don't want to commit that blunder!'

The shadow laughed. Then he said, 'Roshi has been looking for you all day today.'

'She really thinks I'm some stupid prince.'

'Come. Time is short!' the shadow said, extending his hand to Imran.

'Should I fall into your lap?' Imran said and moved to one side. But the next moment the air was knocked out of him. Someone had hit his head from the back with a hard and heavy object. He stumbled towards the shadow, but fainted before reaching him.

Chapter 14

How does one regain consciousness after fainting? This is beyond the comprehension of the one who has just fainted. Anyway, Imran had no idea about how or when he regained consciousness. But the moment he woke up, he regained control over his faculties immediately.

He was in a spacious and lavishly decorated room. But he was not alone. There were five other men with him. They were wearing long black Chester coats, and their faces were covered with black veils. One of them was skimming through the pages of a book.

'So, mister, what did you find out?' another of them asked him.

Imran recognized his voice. He was the same person whom Imran had talked to a short while ago.

'Yes, you are right,' the other person said, fixing his eyes on the book. 'Ali Imran, MSc, DSc, London... Officer on Special Duty...from the Central Intelligence Bureau.'

'So friend, what do you think?' the villain said, turning to Imran.

'Not MSc, DSc, but MSc, PhD!' Imran said gravely.

'Shut up,' the man roared.

'I am really very stupid. Roshi was right!' Imran murmured as if talking to himself.

'What do you know about us?' the man asked.

'That all of you are veiled women and that you are scaring me for no reason.'

'You won't be able to leave this place alive!' the man thundered.

'Don't worry. I'll leave after I am dead,' Imran said recklessly.

He stared at Imran through his veil for some time. Then he said, 'You'll have to tell me how many of your men are working and where they are posted!'

'Are you guys really serious?' Imran said, feigning astonishment.

No one said anything. Their silence was frightening at that moment.

Imran said, 'There has definitely been some misunderstanding!'

'Nonsense...! Our files are compiled very carefully!' the man said.

'Then I guess I'm wrong,' Imran said dejectedly. 'But that's strange... I mean, *me*? Wow! That's wonderful. Can't I do better?! Friends, it is but cruel of you to associate me with the Intelligence Bureau!'

'We don't have a lot of time!' the unknown man said angrily. 'You have until tomorrow morning. Give me the names and addresses of your men, or else...!'

'I think,' one of the veiled persons cut in, 'we should use the hot iron trick. What do you say?'

'There's no time,' the man roared. 'We will see tomorrow.'

They all left the room, locking the door behind them. Imran stretched his arms for a while. He touched the part of his head where he'd been hit and grimaced.

He had not expected the attack. He had thought that he'd already trapped the criminals. He hadn't told them about Hoopoe without a reason. He had a plan and he had succeeded in carrying it out too. By following the person who had photographed Hoopoe at the coast he had identified at least one of the criminals' hideouts... And it was there that he had seen the man with the lopped-off ear.

Imran lay motionless in the easy chair for some time. His mind was rapidly assessing the situation at hand. Half an hour passed. A deep silence hung over the place. Not a single sound could be heard.

Imran got up and began examining the windows and doors. It was soon clear to him that he could not escape by any means. All the doors were locked from the outside. Another important question concerned him—was the building empty, or were there other people in it? He wasn't certain about either. It was impossible for him to be alone in the building. But if there was anyone else other than him in the building, why was it as silent as a cemetery? Were they sleeping? Imran thought it was out of question. It seemed impossible that they were sleeping peacefully especially when they knew that they had caught a dangerous enemy.

Imran knew fully well that they hadn't brought him here to serve him breakfast the next morning.

Neither would they treat him so hospitably that he wouldn't know how to thank them! He got up again and began pacing about the room... Then suddenly he started shouting and banging on the door.

He heard the sound of soft feet and a woman's melodious voice reproached him, 'What's it, why are you making such a racket?'

'I want to get out,' Imran replied very seriously.

'Stop talking nonsense.'

'Shut up!' Imran roared. 'I don't want to talk to a bitch like you... Send a man!'

'Sit quietly, you son of a bitch! Otherwise you'll be shot!'

Imran cursed her loudly. A slew of invective flew out of her mouth in reply. Imran guessed that she was alone in the building. Otherwise she would have definitely called a man to deal with him.

The woman cursed him for a while, and then fell silent. Imran listened to the sound of her feet. He surmised that she had gone to a nearby room.

Imran thought that if he continued to sit here idly, he would surely be remembered by posterity as The Great Idiot. He began examining the room once again. Suddenly he stumbled upon a bundle of rope; he grabbed it quickly. The rope was barely half an inch in diameter. And it looked as if it had been dried after being soaked in water. Imran looked at it for a while. And then a devilish grin lit his face.

Chapter 15

THE WOMAN'S MOOD HAD been ruined when Imran cursed her. She was quite beautiful, about twenty-two years old and it was highly likely that her companions suffered her whims and fancies. Anyway, she did not seem to be the kind who could endure harsh words for too long.

The truth was that she was alone in the building at this time. Imran's captors were perhaps certain that he would not be able to escape from there. Otherwise they would not have committed such a mistake. The enraged woman flung herself on her bed. Perhaps she was also angry with her comrades.

She wanted to sleep. But sleep eluded her. Twenty minutes passed. She kept turning from side to side restlessly. Suddenly she heard a scream from the prisoner's room. And then came other noises—it sounded as if someone was being strangled.

She jumped up instantly and ran towards the prisoner's room. But all was silent now.

'What's the matter? Why are you creating a din?!' she exclaimed when she reached the door.

No one replied. A sliver of light was visible through the gap between the door and its frame.

She peered through the gap, but retreated with a tremendous start, as though she had received an electric shock. The sight that met her eyes gave her goose bumps—a body was hanging from the ceiling! Its feet were swinging three feet above the ground. And a noose was slung around its neck! The face was turned the other way. It was clear that the prisoner had climbed onto a chair, stuck his neck in the noose, and then kicked the chair aside. Clothed in black pants and a long black overcoat, the corpse looked frightful.

She peeped through the crack once again... She couldn't believe her eyes because she had heard a lot about the prisoner's dauntlessness. She couldn't dream or imagine that such a defiant man would commit suicide. Even though he had cursed her a few minutes ago and this had annoyed her very much, she couldn't help feeling despondent at the sight.

She was not a faint-hearted woman. How could a faint-hearted woman live with such dangerous criminals anyway?

She was lost in thought for a while. Then she opened the door and entered the room...

The prisoner's face was turned away from the door. The woman moved forward to look at his face. But before she could reach it, the corpse slipped out of the noose and fell onto the floor. The woman stepped back in amazement. But Imran didn't give her time to escape! In an instant her long, slender neck was in Imran's grip.

'What time will they return?' Imran said, squeezing harder.

The woman swallowed hard. Her eyes were wide open in fear and astonishment, and she was shaking like a leaf.

'Tell me or I'll strangle you!' Imran threatened.

'Half...half past three.'

'You are lying! Fear God and tell the truth or your tongue will burn in hell!' Imran said and let go of her neck.

The woman stood rooted to the spot, trembling.

'You cursed me a short while ago. What do you say now? Should I hack off your ears and nose!'

The girl was silent. Imran continued blabbering. 'You look decent. Otherwise I would have strangled you to death! Are you married to one of them?'

The woman shook her head. Then Imran roared, 'Then who the devil are you? Speak! Or your corpse will be found hanging on this rope!'

'I am not an accomplice in any of their crimes,' the woman said, weeping.

'Then who are you, after all?'

'Whoever I am, here I am. I am fed up of life. They haven't left me with many options. It's impossible for me to now lead a respectable life. But I am desperate to escape their clutches at any cost!'

'Good... Okay, I will save you. But you have to obey my orders.'

'I am willing to do that.'

'Who will open the door when they come? Were you supposed to stay awake until they return?'

'No, they'll open it themselves. And other than them, no one else knows the combination.'

'The exit must be locked from inside?' Imran asked.

'No, it's not locked.'

'Is this the Hirschfield Fisheries building?' Imran asked and the woman nodded.

'This building is on James Street, right?' Imran asked and received an answer in the affirmative to this as well. Imran was satisfied that it was the same building he had followed the photographer to.

He thought for a while and then said, 'Don't try to double-cross me. Go to your room.'

She left quietly for her room. Imran followed her. As soon as she entered her room Imran locked the door from the outside.

'Stay quiet, otherwise you'll be dead. I won't spare you just because you are a woman!' Imran roared.

The woman was quiet. Imran moved ahead. He quickly surveyed the building. He tried opening all the exit doors but they were all locked. He found a hoard of weaponry in a room. The door of the room wasn't locked. Perhaps they had taken a few weapons from the room before leaving and had forgotten to lock the room. Imran picked up a tommy gun, loaded it, and came out of the room, holding the gun in his hand.

Anyone observing Imran's actions would have definitely thought him mentally deranged. He should have called the police so that they could surround the building. There was a phone here. Imran could have used that if he had wanted to. But he didn't. He sniffed every corner of the building like a hound.

It did worry him that the criminals could return any moment now. He was now aware of their crimes and had also figured out the purpose behind that rogue's dominion over the wilderness right by the ABC Hotel.

After a while he returned to the room where he had been locked. He glanced at the woman's room. The door was still locked. The light inside the room had been switched on but he couldn't hear a sound.

Imran looked at the duck clutched in his left hand. He had found the bird in a cage in the building. He entered the room and put the tommy gun on the table. The rope was still hanging from the hoop attached to the ceiling.

Imran slaughtered the duck. Some blood spilled on the floor, and he collected the rest very carefully in a glass.

Chapter 16

THE CENTRAL DOOR OF the building opened at exactly 3 am, and ten people entered the building. The face of only one of them was covered in a veil; the faces of the other nine were uncovered. They looked exhausted.

But the traces of fatigue disappeared from their faces when they saw light emanating from the prisoner's room. Light had spilled out into the lounge through the open door. Their veiled chief ran into the room fearlessly. And then his eyes widened in astonishment. The room was empty. A bloodied rope was hanging from the ceiling...and there was blood on the floor as well... Drops of blood dripping from the rope made a trail to the door... He leaped to the door. His nine aides were standing still and silent at the door.

There were numerous small spots of blood in the lounge. His aides followed the trail of drops.

The trail led to the room with the weapons. One of the men took out a torch from his pocket because the corridor was dark. They found the door of the weapon room wide open. The trail of blood continued around a corner and led straight to the weapon room.

'Oh, a duck! What the...!'

They did not even get a chance to turn around when the door banged shut. Imran's laughter echoed in the dark. But he was unaware that the same darkness which he had taken advantage of could prove deadly for him. He had no idea that someone had been left outside.

Imran hallooed, 'So friends, what do you think now?'

The men began shouting and beating the door from the inside.

Imran laughed loudly again. But his laughter ceased suddenly. Somebody had attacked him from behind. The tommy gun flew out of his hand and fell somewhere in the dark. The assailant was the chief of the gang. While the nine men had been following the trail of blood their chief had paused before the prisoner's room. The rest of them had trooped into the weapon storage room while the chief had stood looking around in apprehension.

And now...perhaps fate was laughing at Imran. It was a fierce attack. Imran felt as though a heavy mountain had fallen on him. Though he was fairly strong, this attack had set his teeth on edge. The veiled man had him in an iron grip.

Imran tried to slip out of his grasp but failed. He was almost suffocating.

There was still a clamour inside the storage room.

'Stay quiet,' the chief censured his men. His voice was as calm as though he was lying indolently on an easy chair.

He yanked Imran up and slowly lifted him off the ground. Imran tried to entangle his legs with his but could not.

There was no doubt that right now Imran was becoming exceedingly anxious and nervous. A madness seemed to have come over the attacker. He was trying to hurl Imran against a wall and crush his bones to powder. He had perhaps forgotten that Imran could easily grab his neck from this position.

If such dangerous criminals do not lose their reason once in a while, as in this case, then the law would be reduced to being a mere relic in a museum showcase—all show and no go.

Imran's hand came into contact with the veiled man's neck, and the drowning man found a straw. Imran clutched the man's neck tightly and both of them came crashing to the floor.

Imran lost his grip on the veiled man's neck but as they fell, Imran elbowed the man on the nose, and punched him on the forehead with his right fist so powerfully that a scream burst out of the veiled man's mouth.

Imran did not want this opportunity to slip out of his hands. He swooped down and grabbed both of the man's hands. The veiled man had fallen on his back and Imran was now sitting on his chest, exerting all his strength to keep the attacker's hands pinned to the ground. His tactic seemed to be working, but he was not free from danger even in this position—Imran had already gauged the veiled man's power, and he knew very well that he could fling Imran away like a ball at the slightest chance.

In a frenzy, Imran hit the veiled man's face with his head. The veiled man was hit on the nose and he writhed in pain. That was it! And then there was no stopping Imran...! The veiled man's screams were frightful. His aides began shouting again, but their leader's voice was gradually reduced to soft moans and groans.

Chapter 17

THE NEXT DAY NOT a single copy of the evening newspaper remained unsold.

Roshi also had a newspaper before her and her eyes were wide open in astonishment. Ali Imran...Imran...she thought...that idiot...was a fearless officer of the Intelligence Bureau!

It was inconceivable that he had arrested a dangerous criminal and his several aides all by himself. And what a criminal he had arrested! One who had harassed the local police for months—had a private telephone exchange, several bungalows in the city, and was a big smuggler! He had several warehouses in which the police had discovered illegally imported priceless goods. He was apparently a modest fisherman and an employee on a steamer of Hirschfield Fisheries. That is, he was the owner of the steamer but the steamer's captain considered him his subordinate. He was the owner of the Hirschfield firm but the firm's manager was blissfully unaware of his very existence—of course, why would the manager know of an insignificant boatman.

He was their boss when he had a black veil on his face. And when he was the boss, the three steamers of Hirschfield Fisheries ferried smuggled goods instead of fish. They loaded illegal goods from foreign ships about fifty miles from the coast and returned to the port. The naval police did not have a clue because the goods were hidden in the lower parts of the ship, and only heaps of fish were visible on the top deck.

This was what was reported in the newspaper, but the truth was that the naval police had a cordial relationship with the Hirschfield staff. Of course, strict surveillance was out of the question.

The news report also explained why that man had terrorized that specific area of wilderness in front of the ABC Hotel. The reason was that smuggled goods were transported to his warehouses through that wilderness. Therefore to keep the area clear, that thug—whose left ear was lopped in half—had on purpose spilled the blood of people who ventured there. The outcome was that the police had had to put up a signboard to warn people of the lurking danger.

The news report also clarified that the ABC Hotel staff had nothing to do with these goings-on.

Roshi gazed at the newspaper for a very long time. On hearing a slight noise she turned towards the door with a start—Imran was standing at the door, beaming at her.

Roshi stood up, baffled. Her face flushed and she lowered her eyes.

'I have struck a deal for fifty buffaloes!'

Roshi did not say anything. Tears fell from her eyes onto her skirt. Even before she had picked up the newspaper, she had had Imran on her mind. And in the past two days she had hunted high and low for him in every corner of the city.

'You are crying...come on,' Imran said, moving towards her.

'Please leave! Leave...!' Roshi said, raising her hand. 'I don't have the energy to be fooled any more!'

'Roshi, tell me honestly.' Imran became serious immediately. 'Did I meet you on purpose? I had no plans to include you in any of my investigations.'

'But why have you come here now?'

'To thank you! And there is one more thing. You once said that you were fed up with your current way of life. Therefore I have come to give you a piece of advice.'

'Advice? I know!' Roshi said dryly. 'You will now say: spend your life in an honourable way! Spare me of the favour of your advice! Ignominious people, like me, also often think that they should spend their lives honourably but it's seldom possible!'

'I want to take you with me!' Imran said. 'My section needs a lady. You will be given a decent pay.'

Roshi's face flushed. She stared at Imran for a while, then said, 'I am in!'

'Haha,' Imran laughed foolishly. 'Now I am taking a thousand buffaloes with me!'

A slight smile appeared on Roshi's lips.

'You really look very sad,' Imran said.

'No...no...not at all!' She forced a laugh.

They remained silent for a while. Then Roshi said, 'There is one thing...'

'One...? Say ten things...but say something!'

'I won't follow the code of conduct when it comes to you. I won't regard you as my boss.'

'Will you call me Parrot? Huh?' Imran said, rolling his eyes.

Roshi began laughing. But she was clearly embarrassed.

'But how did you solve the case at all? I haven't been able to understand that yet!'

'This wasn't detective work, Joshi...er...Roshi! That's commonly called bundlebazi...ummm, bungling, you know, and that's how I get my work done! The art of detection is something much loftier. But this case was one in which that art would have fallen flat on its face. And the truth is that I have actually been fooled in this case.'

'How come?'

'I thought I was fooling them. But when I was trapped in their lair, I realized I was the father of all fools... Okay, wait. Let me tell you before you ask me all the details... Actually, I wanted to give them the impression that I was also a scoundrel like them and that I dealt in counterfeit money. This way I expected to mix with them freely. Well, true to my expectations, their chief invited me to the same wilderness where I was initially attacked.'

'But, tell me, why did you need to pull this trick when you already knew who their chief was?! You asked me about that man with the maimed ear, didn't you?'

'Yes, I did. But I didn't know until then that he was their boss. And then, what good does *knowing* do! I couldn't have laid my hands on him without furnishing evidence against him. And to furnish evidence against them there couldn't have been a better way than the one that I adopted... Yes, so when I reached the place they really took care of me, didn't they?! Haha. That bump on my head is still hurting...! Then they took me to their quarters... And there I learnt that the chief was well aware of my identity!'

Imran told her the story of his 'suicide'. 'I tied the rope around my back, passed it under my overcoat, and wrapped it around my neck in such a way that it looked like a noose from afar—Haha! And then she was trapped!'

'Yeah, you only know how to fool women!' Roshi said, making a face.

'I am a fool myself, Roshi. Believe me! It's only occasionally that I am able to convince others that I am not! That's all!'

Then he recounted the episode of the blood trail and Roshi guffawed.

'But...' Imran said, making a sour face, 'I was fooled here too! I had locked all his goons but he was left outside! And then the truth is that, Roshi, I can't really tell now if I am Imran or not...'

'What!'

'I am Imran's ghost! And if I am not a ghost then it will take me some time to believe that I am still alive. Gosh! Don't know of how much horsepower that wretched man was... No, not horse, but elephant-power, I should say! I didn't think I would be able to save myself. Thank God I had my wits about me, otherwise he would have hurled me like a football!'

Imran fell silent and began chewing his gum.

'Now I am sure that you are really stupid!'

'I am, right? Haha,' Imran guffawed.

'Certainly! No sensible man on earth would have tried to deal with them on his own. You had all the time in the world. You could have contacted the police after getting out of the room!'

'Well, you are right... But in that case we wouldn't have caught even a glimpse of them. It was not some ordinary gang, Roshi. Think about it. A swarm of policemen... God save us... It would have ruined the whole game! Phew! Anyway...! But I know for sure that Daddy is definitely going to call me to account for this and then I might have to resign.'

'Then why are you taking me along?' Roshi asked.

'Don't worry! We will become publishers of detective novels! You can be a street pedlar for those and I'll write to the agents telling them that we will offer them 50 per cent commission upon ordering even a single book! And we can offer to send them the sample cover page a month in advance! If they want they can sell the cover for a rupee and dump the book with a junk seller...' And on and on chattered Imran.

Acknowledgements

I need to thank a number of people for this project. My foremost thanks are to my dear friend and mentor Musharraf Ali Farooqi, the bright star of Urdu translation, without whom this project—and many others—would not have begun.

I am grateful to Ahmad Safi, who, thanks to the dark, power-less evenings of Karachi, literally burnt the midnight oil to compare the text to the Urdu original and suggest his insightful changes. Thanks also to my editor Priyanka Sarkar and copyeditor Rimli Borooah, who did a wonderful job of ironing out the kinks in the text.

I am thankful to my extremely generous and fantastic friend Krupa, who spared the time from her impossible fifteen-hour days to meticulously read the text—and make editorial suggestions. Thanks also to another close friend, Zahra, who was more excited about this project than I, and pressed me untiringly to start and then finish the work in time.

Lastly, but most importantly, many thanks to my family, who bear with my unusual work habits, support me through my intentional joblessness, and always wish me well. In brief, this translation would not have been possible without the help of these wonderful people, whose support has seen me through the darkest hours.

A Note on the Translator

Taimoor Shahid is a writer and a translator. His other book-length work includes a co-translation of a novella, *The Madness of Waiting: The Story of Mirza Ruswa,* by Mirza Hadi Ruswa. He is currently working on the translation of a war account and his first collection of poetry, among other things.